"You've never had a boyfriend?"

He eyed her disbelievingly.

Just the one. Simon. But he had died. And she hadn't allowed herself to love anyone since him.

Liam's mouth twisted. "You seem to be taking a long time finding an answer to that question," he taunted.

She drew in a deep, steadying breath. She had no intention of owning up to a boyfriend, because she had no intention of talking about Simon. Certainly not to this man.

"Why is my personal life of interest to you, Liam?" She used his first name deliberately now, the familiarity putting them back on an equal footing. "Our discussion is merely on a business level," she reminded him firmly.

He calmly met the challenge in her gaze. "I like to know all there is to know about the people I do business with."

For the attention of the Reader

Dear Madam,

Re: **9 to 5**

We have pleasure in drawing your attention to our new series of stories with company settings. You have written to us at Harlequin Presents on many occasions to tell us how much you enjoy office romances. So, it is at the top of our agenda to give you six sizzling months of business affairs.

Because you're the boss and we work to give you nothing but the best, the first vacancy in the **9 to 5** series is filled by your very favorite author, Carole Mortimer. We can guarantee that her story of Juliet and Liam, as they struggle to save their company and not to fall for each other, will entertain and enthrall you right to its very end.

9 to 5: it's the business!

Sincerely,

The Editor

CAROLE MORTIMER

Two's Company

Harlequin Books

TORONTO • NEW YORK • LONDON
AMSTERDAM • PARIS • SYDNEY • HAMBURG
STOCKHOLM • ATHENS • TOKYO • MILAN
MADRID • WARSAW • BUDAPEST • AUCKLAND

ISBN 0-373-11823-6

TWO'S COMPANY

First North American Publication 1996.

CHAPTER ONE

'YOU'RE standing in the way of my view.'

Juliet turned towards the source of the voice, startled out of her early morning reverie by its intrusion, even more startled when she saw the man frowning across at her as he lay on a lounger on the patio a short distance away.

She had been totally unaware of anyone else's presence as she stood near the sea-shore staring out across the calm water, the beauty of the sunrise reflected on that water also lost on her as she wondered how much longer she was going to have to stay here. To most people it wouldn't have been a hardship to stay on at this exclusive hotel on the paradise island of Majorca, but Juliet wasn't most people, and she wasn't here to enjoy herself!

And she certainly wasn't in the mood to put up with what she considered to be this man's rudeness; he might have paid to stay in this hotel too—as she knew, very much so!—but the cost of his hotel suite didn't give him exclusive rights to the view.

Grey eyes surrounded by long dark lashes flashed a warning of her displeasure at being attacked in this way. 'I thought the view belonged to everyone,' she snapped back, putting up a hand to push the heavy swath of her blazing red hair back over her shoulder, having left her own suite earlier without bothering to secure it at her nape as she usually did.

She had been on the island almost a week now, and she found the nights the most difficult to deal with. She had no trouble keeping herself occupied during the day, but at night she would fall into a troubled sleep for a couple of hours, and then wake up at about three o'clock in the morning unable to go back to sleep again. She had taken to going for long walks along the sea-shore as soon as it became light, and this morning had been no exception.

Two more days, she had decided on this morning's walk, and then she would give up her vigil and go back home to England. She was solving absolutely nothing by staying on here anyway; the person she had come here to see just wasn't going to put in an appearance, and she might as well accept that.

The man stood up from the lounger, tall and lithe in a black T-shirt and fitted denims, his over-long hair glinting golden in the sunshine, eyes the blue of the water lapping in front of them, and squinted in the bright early morning sun as he stared across the width of his patio-area at her.

It was only just after six o'clock in the morning, too early for any of the other hotel guests to be up and about, and Juliet was suddenly aware, as the man walked towards her, of just how alone the two of them were. And he didn't exactly sound friendly, either; in fact, he was distinctly hostile!

As he came to stand just in front of her Juliet realised exactly how tall he was, dwarfing her five feet two in height by at least a foot, making her even more conscious of her own vulnerability alone on the sea-shore with him.

'The view does belong to everyone,' he murmured in that husky voice. 'I was just surprised to see someone else out and about this early in the morning.'

And that gave him the right to be rude to her? As far as apologies went it wasn't exactly effusive, but then this man gave the impression of rarely, if ever, making apologies for anything!

Up close like this he looked to be in his late thirties, had a ruggedly handsome face, dark lashes surrounding those sharply alert blue eyes, his nose long and straight, his mouth a sculptured curve, the chin square and powerful. And he was looking down that long nose at her now, no matter how pleasant his words just now might have sounded.

Juliet shrugged, her own clothing similar to his except that the T-shirt tucked into the narrow waistband of her jeans was navy blue in colour. She looked very small and slight next to his much more forceful physique.

'The morning is the most beautiful part of the day,' she dismissed—although at three o'clock in the morning she hadn't been quite so sure about that!

'I happen to agree,' he nodded, still looking at her with those piercing blue eyes—eyes that seemed to miss nothing.

For all that he was dressed casually he didn't look like the usual holiday-makers Juliet had so far seen at this exclusive hotel. Most of them, including the men, were more interested in making a fashion statement with their clothing than actually relaxing and enjoying the sun and the sea, and this man gave the impression that he didn't give a damn about fashion, that he dressed for comfort, and to hell with what anyone else thought about the way he looked. Even that slightly waving golden-coloured hair was unfashionably long. Although she could be making a complete misjudgement—she very often did—and later on, when he was joined by his fashion-conscious wife and spoilt teenage children, she would know that she had!

'Well, if you'll excuse me...' She gave him a bright dismissive smile before turning away.

'No,' he said abruptly from behind her.

Juliet turned with a frown; what did he mean, no?

'I ordered coffee a few minutes ago,' he smiled, revealing even white teeth, his eyes crinkling at the corners.

It was amazing the difference that smile made to his face; he no longer looked remote and slightly daunting, and certainly not hostile. But, nevertheless, Juliet was still somewhat perplexed by his manner.

'Why don't you join me?' he offered smoothly.

Her grey eyes widened. Really, she had just met the man, and he had been distinctly rude from the first, and now he had the nerve to ask her to join him for coffee. 'Wouldn't your wife think that rather odd?' she returned with sweet sarcasm.

She had kept herself very much to herself since her arrival here, resisted all the attempts of the other guests to try and include her in their activities. She was very much a loner anyway, so that hadn't been difficult for her to do; she certainly had no intention of joining this man for coffee—or anything else.

His mouth twisted. 'I don't have a wife,' he told her drily. 'And even if I did I can't see anything wrong in my asking you to join me for a cup of coffee!'

Colour warmed Juliet's cheeks at what she sensed was his mockery. Maybe she was being a little over-cautious, but her experiences of life so far had taught her to have very little trust in other people—especially some lone man she had accidentally met like this.

'I don't——'

'Could you put the tray on the table, please? And bring another cup.' The golden-haired stranger talked past Juliet and over her shoulder, and as she turned she could see the waiter arriving with his tray of coffee things. In fact, it wasn't just coffee; there were rolls and croissants there too.

And he was obviously a man used to giving orders and expecting them to be obeyed, she thought as she watched the waiter putting the tray down on the table on the patio before going off to get the second cup.

'Come and sit down,' he offered now, strolling back on to his patio with long, easy strides. 'Would you like something to eat?' He indicated the rolls and croissants. 'There's plenty here for two.'

Juliet gave him a perplexed frown. She hadn't exactly got around to refusing his offer of coffee, but it must have been obvious to him that she had been about to do so when the waiter arrived. And yet he was choosing to ignore that. He had also put her in a position where it would look very churlish of her to refuse the offer now.

She joined him on the patio to his suite with some reluctance, the man waiting to resume his seat until she had made herself comfortable in one of the four chairs arranged around the table, and choosing the one directly to her left rather than the one opposite which she had been hoping he would opt for.

'Nothing to eat for me, thank you,' she refused stiltedly, not exactly comfortable with this situation; she felt as if she had been coerced into it, and it didn't sit well with her normally self-sufficient nature.

He gave her a considering look. 'You look as if a few pounds in weight wouldn't do you any harm.' He arched pointed brows at her almost boyish figure.

Juliet was well aware of the fact that she was probably more slender now than she had ever been in her twenty-seven years, and that it didn't exactly suit her to be this thin, but she certainly didn't appreciate this man telling her so. 'Just coffee, thanks,' she told him abruptly, intending to drink up as quickly as possible and make her escape.

But as he nodded before pouring the steaming hot brew into the waiting cup she knew that that wasn't going to be immediately possible, not unless she wanted to make a complete idiot of herself by scalding her mouth in her haste! She added plenty of cream when he placed the cup in front of her, but even so she knew it was still going to be too hot to drink just yet.

'I'm Liam, by the way.' He looked at her enquiringly.

'Juliet,' she muttered into her cup, just as unforthcoming, before taking a hesitant sip of the steaming liquid. It was as hot as she had suspected, and she put the cup back down again, resigned to spending more time than she wanted in this man's company.

'Thanks.' He smiled dismissively at the waiter as he arrived with the other cup and saucer. 'Are you here on business or pleasure?'

Juliet looked up at him sharply as she realised that he was once again talking to her. 'Business?' she echoed tautly.

He shrugged broad shoulders, relaxing back in his chair. 'There are plenty of business opportunities here. Even this hotel is up for sale.'

And she hardly looked in a position to buy one of the Carlyle hotels! 'So I believe,' she answered non-committally. 'Is that why you're here?' she returned challengingly.

He shook his head. 'This is purely a pleasure trip for me. I was just curious about you; you don't look the usual type to book into an adventure playground like this one.' He raised questioning brows at her.

Juliet bristled with indignation. What 'type' did she look? Oh, he was right, of course, but even so...!

And he hardly looked like the bored socialite in search of the sun—a description which seemed to fit most of the guests here. 'It seemed like a good idea at the time.' She shrugged dismissively.

Liam nodded. 'Thinking about a holiday and actually taking one are two different things, aren't they?' he said drily.

'But you've only just arrived here—I mean, I haven't seen you around for the last week,' she ex-

plained awkwardly, that colour back in her cheeks
as she realised that she had given away the fact that
he was the sort of man she would have noticed if
she had seen him before. But she would have done;
he was hardly the type of man to be overlooked in
a crowd, let alone here at this hotel! Nevertheless,
she felt a little embarrassed at having acknowledged the fact.

'I arrived last night. As you said, it seemed like
a good idea at the time,' he added grimly. 'Now
I'm not so sure.'

'You've hardly given yourself time,' Juliet
pointed out.

Liam looked at her over the rim of his coffee-
cup, having ignored the cream and sugar to drink
it black. 'How long have you been here?' he
drawled.

She shrugged. 'Almost a week.'

'And?' He arched blond brows.

She suddenly realised the point he was making.
'I didn't come here with the intention of enjoying
myself,' she snapped irritably.

He sat back once again. 'No? Then you *are* here
on business?'

This man was altogether too curious, too
probing, too damned direct! 'Perhaps,' she returned non-committally, trying the coffee once
again, just wanting to drink it and be on her way
back to her own suite of rooms.

'I'm not that daunting, am I?'

She looked up sharply to find that Liam was
watching her, amusement dancing in those deep
blue eyes now as he looked pointedly at the half-
empty cup in her hand. Juliet put the cup back in

its saucer with a clatter. 'I think I should get back to my suite now. I would like to shower and change before breakfast,' she told him stiltedly.

He nodded. 'Join me for lunch?'

She stiffened defensively. 'No, I——'

'We're both on our own, Juliet,' he cut in reasonably. 'It's ridiculous for the two of us to eat alone.'

She stood up abruptly, her hair falling loosely over her narrow shoulders, a blaze of red in the sunshine. 'I prefer to eat alone, thank you,' she snapped. 'And I'm certainly not here for a pickup!' She was breathing hard in her agitation.

Liam appeared unmoved by her outburst, looking at her consideringly. 'I didn't for one moment think that you were,' he finally said softly.

Juliet gave him one last frowning look before turning on her heel and hurrying away across the garden to the main entrance of the hotel, very conscious as she did so that he was watching every step of her departure.

She began to breathe easily again once she was inside the reception area, although the haste of her steps didn't lessen as she hurried over to the lift and waited impatiently for its arrival to the ground floor. Not that she thought for one moment that the man, Liam, would follow her; she just felt completely disturbed by the whole encounter, wanted to get to the privacy of her own suite as quickly as possible so that she could begin to relax her jangled nerves.

Not that Liam had been the first man to show some sort of interest in her since her arrival here. There had been several other single men in the complex who had obviously seen her as a prime

target for a holiday romance, although she hadn't
thought any of them particularly had romance in
mind, more like a bed-partner for the duration of
their stay! But she hadn't been interested in any of
their overtures, and she certainly wasn't interested
in Liam's either.

It wasn't that he wasn't an attractive man—she
would be fooling herself if she didn't acknowledge
that—but she wasn't interested in a relationship of
any kind, of any duration, with anyone.

She had come here for quite a different reason,
and after six days of waiting she had to accept that
it had been a wasted journey. It had been made out
of desperation anyway—a last-ditch attempt to
locate and talk to Edward Carlyle before it was too
late. The problem was that he had made it very
clear that he didn't want to talk to her, that he had
nothing to say to her, and it had been a purely ac-
cidental comment, made by the secretary she had
plagued for days for information of his whereabouts, which had made it possible for her to know
that he would be on the island of Majorca at this
time to meet a prospective buyer for his hotel. This
hotel.

Instead of showering and changing as she had
said she was going to she lay on the bed staring up
at the pristine white ceiling. Time was running out,
and she just didn't know what to do to stop everything collapsing around her ears. Edward Carlyle
was the key, she knew that, but she also knew he
had every intention of letting things collapse.

She had never met the man, but she knew of him
from his father, William, knew that the two men
had argued years before, with Edward leaving the

family and the family business with a vow never to
return to either. And now that family business was
in danger of falling. Without Edward Carlyle's in-
tervention, that was exactly what it was going to
do. And so far he had proved impervious to her
request that the two of them should meet to discuss
the matter.

She had been stunned when on William's death
two months ago, his will had revealed that he had
left Carlyle Properties jointly between Juliet and
his remaining son Edward, his younger son having
died several years earlier. As William's personal assistant Juliet obviously knew how to run the
company, but with a completely joint ownership
between herself and Edward Carlyle, an exact fifty-
fifty split, it was impossible for her to make any
major decisions without the approval of the other
partner. And Edward Carlyle refused even to acknowledge her letters, let alone come to England
and talk over the running of the business.

It was deliberate, Juliet was sure of that. She
knew that even though his father was now dead
Edward Carlyle must still harbour feelings of anger
towards William, that the family rift was still there
despite the death of one of the participants. Edward
Carlyle was going to let his father's property
business fail simply by being indifferent to its
existence!

Obviously, with the success of his own chain of
exclusive hotels all over the world, Edward Carlyle
didn't need Carlyle Properties, but Juliet felt a sense
of loyalty to William to keep the company going.
He had done so much for her, she didn't want to
let him down now...

She had tried what had amounted almost to camping out in Edward Carlyle's head office in England, the luxurious suite of offices from where he supposedly ran the hotel chain. But it had transpired that he spent little time there, preferring to be actually in the hotels themselves to ensure their efficient running.

And no wonder, if this hotel complex was anything to go by; in the six days Juliet had been here she had quickly realised how easy it would be to become used to the attentive luxury of a place like this! There was everything one could possibly need here to ensure every comfort. Except Edward Carlyle himself!

Unfortunately the property business was still a difficult thing to be in, and William had only just managed to salvage the company three years before when the market had collapsed around a lot of people's ears. Things were starting to pick up again now for anyone who had actually survived that collapse, but, even so, decisions still had to be made very carefully. And without Edward Carlyle's agreement Juliet couldn't make any at all....

She turned over on the bed with a pained groan. She had to find Edward Carlyle. She just had to. Two more days and she would go back to England and start her search for him all over again. While there was still time she wasn't about to give up. She couldn't! She owed it to William not to...

She hadn't even been aware of dozing off, but she knew that she must have been asleep for some time when she rolled over on the bed to see the bright sunshine blazing through the doors that led out to the balcony of this first-floor suite. A quick glance at her watch revealed that it was after eleven o'clock. Almost lunchtime, and she hadn't even had breakfast yet!

As usual, there was a buffet lunch being set out in one of the gardens when Juliet ventured downstairs almost an hour later, having showered and changed into a cotton sundress of a bright red colour that somehow managed not to clash with the blaze of her now confined hair, a tortoiseshell slide loosely securing its curling length at her nape. It had been strange, a week ago in England, packing all her summer things to bring away with her; in early November in England it was already cold and wintry.

The man, Liam, was the last person she wanted to see as she approached one of the tables placed about the garden near the buffet. He was seated at another table a short distance away, watching her with narrowed blue eyes, still wearing the faded denims but having put on a short-sleeved shirt of the same sky-blue colour as his eyes. His hair looked even more golden in the bright midday sun, his skin tanned a dark bronze.

No doubt, like a lot of the other guests here, he spent a great deal of time sitting around in the sun doing nothing but improving his tan, Juliet thought disgruntledly as she put her laden plate down on the table and sat down abruptly, carefully avoiding looking across at Liam as she did so.

She no longer felt hungry as she looked down at the salad and fruit on her plate. What was she doing here? This wasn't her sort of place at all; these weren't her sort of people either. God, it was all such a waste of time, and——

'I should eat that if I were you,' murmured a familiar voice from above her. 'You look as if a puff of wind might blow you away!' Liam added grimly.

Juliet had looked up at him at the first sound of his voice, and her face became flushed with irritation now as she heard his last comment. 'I would hardly have selected the food if I didn't intend eating it,' she bit out tautly, deliberately picking up her fork at his taunt to stab at a piece of melon and put it pointedly in her mouth, meeting his gaze challengingly once she had done so.

'Fruit and salad . . .' He was shaking his head as he lowered his lean length into the seat next to her. 'It's hardly going to pile on the pounds, is it?'

She swallowed the piece of melon, almost choking on it as she realised she had forgotten to chew it. 'I don't want to "pile on the pounds", thank you!' she finally managed to snap.

Liam sat forward, his elbows resting on the table beside her, the hair on his tanned arms a golden blond too. 'It may be fashionable to be thin, Juliet,' he said softly, 'but most men prefer a woman they can actually hold on to.'

She gasped at his familiarity; didn't this man know how to take a hint? It must be perfectly obvious to him by now that she didn't appreciate his intrusive company. God, she had told him bluntly enough that she wasn't in the market to be picked up. But maybe that fact alone was a challenge to him, she wearily acknowledged; he looked like the sort of man who would relish any sort of challenge offered to him!

Well, she had said it, and she meant it; she had much more important things to do here than become the plaything of a man like Liam. 'I really don't care what "most men prefer",' she told him with sweet venom. 'Now, if you wouldn't mind, I would like to eat my lunch in peace.' She looked at him pointedly.

'Don't mind me.' He relaxed back in his chair, folding his arms across his chest to watch her with narrowed blue eyes.

That was hardly what she had meant and he knew it! What was she supposed to do now? Because she had no intention of eating her lunch with this man sitting there watching her every move.

'You——' She broke off, looking past him to the table where he had been sitting minutes earlier.

A woman was now sitting at the table, looking across at the two of them enquiringly—a beautiful woman who looked to be in her mid-thirties, her blonde hair short but perfectly styled, make-up expertly applied. And she was obviously waiting for Liam... He hadn't wasted much time since his arrival here; breakfast with Juliet, lunch with this other woman! And the other woman, with her slightly voluptuous figure, looked exactly the sort of woman a man could hold on to!

Juliet turned back to Liam. 'I believe your luncheon guest has just arrived,' she informed him directly.

He turned to glance casually over at his table, lifting his hand to the woman in an acknowledging salute, before turning back to Juliet. 'Perhaps I'll see you later,' he said huskily as he stood up to leave.

Not if she saw him first! Avoiding this persistent man was going to make these last two days of her stay even more of a trial than the previous six had been. But maybe not, she thought with a grimace as she saw the way the beautiful blonde woman looked up and smiled at him as he joined her at the table; he looked as if he might have his time filled quite adequately by her. Thank God!

Men, especially of the type she guessed Liam to be, were not something she wanted in her life. She didn't want any man in her life!

Except Edward Carlyle. She desperately needed to have him in her life, in the life of Carlyle Properties—otherwise there wasn't going to be a company at all.

That thought put her totally off eating any more of her lunch, and she put the fork down, the food untouched—except for that piece of melon she had so defiantly eaten when Liam had been sitting with her.

She wanted to leave, having totally lost her appetite, but she was very conscious of the fact that if she did so Liam would no doubt watch her going.

What difference did it make if Liam watched her leave? she irritably admonished herself, standing up determinedly; it was none of his business whether or not she ate her lunch!

She walked past the table where he sat with the attractive blonde woman, her head held high. Deep in conversation with his luncheon companion, he didn't even glance her way.

And Juliet was even more annoyed with herself for even thinking that he would have noticed her departure!

There was something so very beautiful about Majorca in the evening. The sunset brought into focus all the beauty of the orange-pink stonework of the buildings that were prevalent on this lovely island, of the hotel itself as Juliet walked along the sea-shore towards it on her way to dinner, bathed in the pink glow of sunset.

If only she could be like the other carefree holiday-makers here just wanting to enjoy themselves. But it seemed like years since she had been carefree. If she ever had been!

There had been years of being in foster care and then several more years of being out in the world on her own. Before meeting Simon...

At the thought of him she brought her thoughts to an abrupt halt. She hadn't thought of him for years; refused to think of him. It was all too painful...

Then why was she thinking of him now? She frowned. She knew why. That man, Liam, in some way reminded her of Simon. Oh, not in his manner; Liam was much more self-assured and powerful than Simon had ever been. Simon had been so weak. But their colouring was the same; Simon had been blond as Liam, with the same deep blue eyes. He had been almost as tall as the other man too.

Maybe that was one of the reasons why Liam had evoked such a strong response within her; she could usually handle any advances made to her without feeling as if she was running away! But

Liam had made her feel defensive from the first.
And now she knew the reason why. He reminded
her of Simon, the man she had once loved so
deeply...

And, having realised that, Juliet found it was not
conducive to her peace of mind that Liam was the
first person she saw when she entered the hotel
dining-room half an hour later. He was seated alone
at a table near a window that overlooked the
tranquil bay of this beautiful resort in the north of
the island, his luncheon companion noticeably
absent. And he looked devastatingly attractive in a
white dinner-jacket and snowy white shirt with a
white bow-tie, his blond hair brushed back from
his face, his eyes deeply blue against his tan.

Juliet looked quickly away from him because he
seemed to sense her gaze on him and turned in the
direction of the doorway she had just walked
through. Probably he had been expecting the
beautiful blonde from lunch; he was obviously
waiting for someone, as his table was set for two
people. And the other woman would probably want
to make a grand entrance when she did arrive—
unlike Juliet, who just wanted to reach her table as
quickly as possible, away from that piercing blue
gaze which she could feel was watching her every
move now.

The black dress she wore was plain but stylish,
fitting neatly to the smooth contours of her body,
showing the extent of her shapely legs beneath its
knee-length hem. Her hair, the long red curls wilder
than usual from the slight breeze that had blown
up this afternoon, was loosely confined at her nape

with a black slide this time, her make-up light, her lip-gloss a light peach colour.

She had checked her appearance before she'd left her suite, and knew she looked elegantly attractive rather than showily sexy—the way she had always liked to look when she had acted as William's hostess during business dinners. It was a style of dress that made her feel comfortable. But not so with Liam watching her so intently!

She kept her gaze on the back of the *maître d'* as he took her to her table, looking to neither left nor right of the elegant candlelit dining-room as she did so, not wanting even inadvertently to meet the gaze of the man Liam.

'Good evening, Juliet.'

She looked up at the sound of his voice, her eyes widening as she realised that the *maître d'* had left after showing her to the table Liam occupied. Liam was standing now as he looked down at her with amused blue eyes.

She shook her head, colour darkening her cheeks. 'There seems to have been some sort of mistake...' She looked about her self-consciously.

'No mistake, Juliet,' he assured her smoothly, coming around the table to pull back the chair that was placed opposite his.

She frowned up at him, making no move to sit in the chair. 'But I don't want to have dinner with you,' she blurted out bluntly.

'Oh, I think you do, Juliet,' he murmured derisively, that amusement still in his dark blue eyes.

She looked up at him indignantly. 'I most certainly do not!' she snapped. 'What happened to your companion from lunch? Didn't it work out?'

she scorned with obvious sarcasm. Really, this man was extremely arrogant to have assumed that she would be willing to have dinner with him, even going so far as to tell the *maître d'*—obviously, because the other man had shown her to this table without hesitation!—that she would be joining him. Well, she had no intention of doing so!

The amusement gone from his eyes now, his gaze narrowed. 'Sit down, Juliet,' he told her softly, but nevertheless in a voice that brooked no further argument.

No doubt he was uncomfortable with the attention—albeit discreetly—that was being directed their way from the other diners in the room because of her obvious reluctance to join him at his table. Probably this had never happened to him before, Juliet realised disgustedly.

Her gaze was steady as she looked up at him, grey eyes cool and calm. 'I told you, I don't want to have dinner with you,' she said evenly, her voice lowered.

Liam straightened, his expression grim now. 'And if you remember I said that you do,' he returned challengingly.

Her eyes widened now. He really was the most...! 'Maybe this arrogant approach works with some women,' she snapped indignantly, 'but it certainly isn't going to work with me! Now, if you'll excuse me...?' She looked at him pointedly as he stood firmly in the way of her walking away from the table.

'Certainly.' He stepped back. 'But I was under the impression,' he added softly as she turned away, 'that you wanted to talk to me.'

Juliet turned back dazedly. 'I can't imagine how you ever gained that impression,' she said incredulously. 'Other than bluntly telling you I don't care whether I ever set eyes on you again, I've done everything I could to show you that I'm not interested in whatever you have in mind. You really do have the most monumental arrogance, Mr... Liam!' Her eyes flashed her anger as she glared up at him.

'The name is Carlyle, Juliet,' he told her softly. 'Edward *William* Carlyle,' he added pointedly. 'Are you still of the opinion that you don't care whether you ever set eyes on me again?' He coolly returned her gaze, his brows raised mockingly.

CHAPTER TWO

JULIET didn't have to be asked to sit down again; she almost fell into the waiting chair, all the time looking up at the man she now knew to be Edward Carlyle, the man she had come here to see.

He was Edward Carlyle. Edward *William* Carlyle, that middle name obviously where the Liam part came from. Good God, she still couldn't believe it. He had been this close to her all day and she hadn't even known it.

But he had known exactly who she was, she suddenly realised as she watched him resume his seat in the chair opposite her. And he had been playing some sort of cat-and-mouse game with her all day...

And he still was, she slowly acknowledged as he met her gaze coolly across the width of the table that stood between them. He looked perfectly relaxed as he rested the lean length of his body back in the chair.

Juliet drew in a slow, controlling breath. She had found Edward Carlyle at last or rather he had found *her*! She mustn't let her feelings of resentment at his subterfuge override her need to speak with him. But she did feel resentful; there was no doubt about it. He had known all along exactly who she was, she was sure of that now, but he had chosen not to let her know who he was until he had been ready to do so. Which appeared to be now.

'You're right,' she nodded, amazed at how calm she sounded considering that she still felt slightly dazed by the fact that she had already had at least two other opportunities today to speak to Edward Carlyle, and hadn't even been aware of it. 'I do want to speak to you. I——'

'Shall we order dinner first?' he suggested lightly as the waiter appeared at their table.

The last thing she felt like doing now was eating; in fact, she felt as if food might actually choke her. 'I haven't had a chance to look at the menu yet,' she said awkwardly.

Liam—Edward Carlyle—gave her a considering look. 'Would you like me to order for you?' he offered distantly. 'I can recommend the salmon and the pork.'

He should be able to—he owned the damned hotel! God! Ordinarily she would have told him what he could do—what any man could do!—with his arrogance in suggesting that he order her food for her, but there was nothing ordinary about this meeting, and quite frankly she didn't feel up to choosing anything for herself. 'Fine,' she accepted abruptly, closing her unread menu before turning to stare sightlessly out of the window while he spoke to the waiter.

This wasn't at all how she had envisaged meeting Edward Carlyle; she had thought it would be on a business footing, not the two of them sitting here in evening clothes about to eat a meal together. Especially when, until a few minutes ago, one of them had been at a complete disadvantage in not knowing exactly whom she was speaking to!

He didn't look anything like William, his father having been dark-haired, with astute grey eyes and softer features than his son's. She could be forgiven for not having made any connection between the two men. But that didn't alter the fact that she was now sitting opposite Edward Carlyle at the meeting she had wanted for the last two months—and that she felt completely at a loss as to how to even begin the conversation they needed to have!

She drew in a ragged breath as she turned back to face him. 'Mr Carlyle——'

'The name is still Liam,' he cut in firmly. 'No one but my father ever called me Edward. And *he* was "Mr Carlyle",' he added grimly.

The friction that had existed between the two men when William had been alive was still obvious in Liam's voice. Juliet sat forward in her seat. 'We need to talk, Mr...Liam,' she amended at his frowning look. 'But I don't think these are exactly the right circumstances.' She looked pointedly around them at the rapidly filling restaurant. A pianist and a violinist were now taking up their positions across the room.

'No,' he acknowledged abruptly as the music began to play softly in the background.

Juliet frowned across the table at him. She was looking at him with new eyes now that she knew he wasn't just a man who had been trying to pick her up for a holiday fling. And she could see a toughness about his mouth and eyes, a power in the hard lines of his face; he didn't look as if he was going to be an easy man to talk to in any circumstances!

'We'll have dinner, Juliet,' he told her softly. 'Then we can talk over coffee in one of the lounges.'

That still wasn't ideal. This was a business affair, not something to be discussed in these luxurious surroundings over a cup of coffee!

'Juliet,' Liam continued firmly as he steadily met her gaze across the width of the table, 'we do this on my terms or not at all.'

Her eyes flashed, deeply grey. He knew that he had the upper hand and was very much in control of the situation. And he was enjoying the power.

But if she got up and walked out now would he ever give her the opportunity to talk to him again? Somehow she knew that he wouldn't. He didn't need to; he had already shown his lack of interest in Carlyle Properties. If she wanted to talk to him at all, she was going to have to sit here and suffer through dinner with him. But for what reason? If they didn't discuss business, what else were they going to talk about for the couple of hours it would take to eat the meal?

'Tell me about yourself, Juliet,' he invited once their salmon had been delivered to the table.

She gave him a startled look. What did he mean, tell him about herself? What was there to tell? He must already know that she was his partner in Carlyle Properties, and he had stated quite firmly that he didn't want to talk about business just yet, so...

'Your personal life, Juliet,' he drawled mockingly, seeing her puzzled expression.

She blinked across at him, making no effort to use the fish-knife and fork she had picked up preparatory to eating her salmon. Personal life? She didn't have one. Carlyle Properties had been her life for the last seven years.

'You must have one,' he taunted, having no hesitation in starting his own meal.

She shook her head. 'No, I——'

'Where do you live? Do you have a family? A boyfriend? Lover? Or are you married? With children?'

The questions were shot at her in such quick-fire succession that Juliet barely had time to draw her breath before Liam delivered the next one. And what he was asking was too personal when they were only business partners!

'I could ask you the same questions,' she returned challengingly.

His mouth twisted mockingly. 'Well, I certainly don't have a boyfriend!'

Her cheeks warmed at his mocking tone. 'I saw your girlfriend earlier,' she snapped irritably.

He frowned slightly, and then his brow cleared. 'You mean Diana,' he nodded. 'Diana isn't my girlfriend, Juliet; she's my personal assistant.'

Juliet gave him a slightly sceptical look from beneath raised brows. If that was what he chose to call the other woman that was up to him, but there had seemed to be a familiarity between the two of them that implied a slightly deeper relationship than the one he had described.

'As you were my father's personal assistant,' he added softly.

Juliet gave him a sharp look, but the blue eyes that returned her gaze were completely enigmatic. Just how much did this man already know about her? And if he already knew the answers to the questions he had asked her why had he asked them at all?

She gave a cool nod of acknowledgement. 'As I was your father's assistant.'

'And now you're his joint heir,' Liam bit out hardly.

She swallowed hard. It must seem strange to William's son that his father had worded his will in the way he had, she freely acknowledged that, and if Liam had shown the slightest interest in Carlyle Properties during the last two months she would gladly have told him that she knew he had prior claim to the company. But she knew from his behaviour that he would be quite happy to see Carlyle Properties go under, and she owed William more than to allow that.

'You didn't answer my question, Juliet,' Liam continued in that hard voice.

'Do I need to?' She met his gaze with a calmness she was far from feeling. 'You seem to know enough about me already. And what you don't know I'm sure you could make up!'

He gave a shrug of indifference at her show of temper, sitting back in his chair, giving up all idea of eating his own food now. 'You live at Carlyle House—have probably done so for some time, even before my father's death?' He raised mockingly questioning brows.

'For several years before that,' she acknowledged tautly.

He pursed his lips. 'And what did your boyfriend make of that?'

God, how he persisted! 'I don't have a boyfriend,' she bit out coldly, so angry that she was starting to shake with the emotion, her eyes flashing, darkly grey.

Blond brows rose. 'At the moment?'

'Ever!' she answered forcefully.

He eyed her disbelievingly. 'You've never had a boyfriend?'

Just the one. Simon. But he had died. And she hadn't allowed herself to love anyone since him.

Liam's mouth twisted. 'You seem to be taking a long time finding an answer to that question,' he taunted.

She drew in a deep, steadying breath, determined not to give him the satisfaction of seeing just how much he was disconcerting her. She had no intention of owning up to a boyfriend, because she had no intention of talking about Simon. Certainly not to this man.

'Why is my personal life of interest to you, Liam?' She used his first name deliberately now, the familiarity putting them back on an equal footing. 'Our discussion is merely on a business level,' she reminded him firmly.

He calmly met the challenge in her gaze. 'I like to know all there is to know about the people I do business with,' he returned softly.

Juliet felt the warmth in her cheeks. She didn't like the idea of this man knowing all there was to know about her; she had lived her life very privately for the last seven years. The fact that she now had a larger-than-life business partner, whose name was synonymous with the exclusivity to be found at his hotels world-wide, couldn't be allowed to change that.

'I'm sorry to disappoint you, Liam,' she bit out tautly, 'but I don't actually have a private life to speak of.'

'A career woman, hmm?'

The way Liam said it, it sounded like an insult! But that was exactly what she was. Oh, not in the way of hard-headed businesswomen who lived for nothing but succeeding and getting ahead, no matter who they had to step on or over to get there. But Carlyle Properties had become the main focus of her life, and in that sense she was a career woman.

'Only as far as Carlyle Properties is concerned,' she told him stiffly, made more and more uncomfortable by this conversation. She had wanted to meet William's son only as a means of keeping the business going, wanted nothing more than a business partnership with him, had no interest in his personal life, and resented the fact that he should take any in hers.

The blue eyes glittered coldly. 'It's interesting that a young woman of twenty-seven, with no surface connection to the Carlyle family, should live in Carlyle House and inherit half the family business...'

It wasn't 'interesting' at all. In fact, now that she had met this man, this whole thing was turning out to be more trouble than it was worth! But she owed William so much...

'Perhaps,' she conceded distantly. 'But as your father's personal assistant——'

'And just how "personal" was that?' Liam watched her across the table with narrowed eyes.

Juliet looked up at him sharply. 'Just what are you implying, Mr Carlyle?' she bit out tautly.

He shrugged broad shoulders. 'My father was old enough to be your grandfather——'

'Hardly, Liam,' she cut in derisively.

'He was sixty-five when he died, Juliet,' he reminded her coldly. 'More than old enough to be your grandfather.'

She had never thought of William in those terms, but, put like that, she supposed that in actual years William could have been her grandfather. But even so...

'Why did you live with him, Juliet?' Liam didn't give her a chance to answer before attacking again. 'Surely that isn't normal in a business association?'

Under attack was exactly how she felt now. This man, for all his apparent lack of emotion about this situation, was obviously not so calm beneath the surface. 'Your father and I were friends as much as anything else,' she returned defensively.

'Close friends?'

She didn't just *feel* under attack now, she *was* under attack! No doubt about it. Liam's eyes glittered dangerously, his mouth a thin, angry line.

She gave up any pretence of trying to eat a meal with him; they were both wasting their time even attempting it under these circumstances. 'I suggest we meet at ten o'clock tomorrow morning in one of the conference-rooms here, Liam,' she told him evenly, bending down to pick up her evening bag. 'We can discuss anything you care to talk about then.'

His eyes were narrowed to ominous blue slits. 'Anything?'

'Within reason,' she nodded.

He shook his head. 'I don't think you're in a position to dictate conditions, Juliet,' he scorned.

Neither did she! But she had a feeling that if she showed this man an ounce of weakness he would use it to his advantage. And to have become as successful as he had over the last ten years he must have had to play by his own set of rules, otherwise he would never have survived in business, let alone have owned his world-wide string of hotel and leisure complexes! She was a mere beginner compared to this man.

'Possibly not,' she conceded, standing up smoothly, her lack of composure not showing by so much as a tremble of her hands as she held on to her evening bag—possibly because she was holding on to that bag so tightly, was gripping the black leather so hard, her hands couldn't tremble! 'But nevertheless I do not conduct business discussions over dinner. And this *is* a business discussion, Liam,' she added firmly. 'And tomorrow when we meet I will bring the necessary paperwork with me so that we can talk knowledgeably about Carlyle Properties.'

He gave her a look that said she could bring the paperwork but whether or not he chose to discuss its contents would be completely up to him!

Juliet was inwardly shaken by that look, but she managed to give him a cool nod before turning and walking from the dining-room, all the time conscious of that narrowed blue gaze following her progress across the room. She'd known it would.

She was still stunned by the realisation that he was Edward Carlyle. She could have had no inkling, no idea—God, she had had no idea! And he had been playing with her all day. No doubt he had enjoyed himself at her expense, but she just felt totally stunned by the whole encounter.

And no wonder meeting Liam had brought back such sharp memories of Simon—the two men had been brothers...!

Neither man had looked in the least like William, and Juliet realised that was because they had both taken after William's blonde-haired, blue-eyed wife—the wife who had died after giving birth to Simon.

Juliet had been nineteen and working in the office of Carlyle Properties as a junior typist when she had met Simon, the twenty-five-year-old son of the owner. And the two of them had been attracted to each other from the start.

At the time Juliet hadn't even realised that Simon had a brother; William and Edward had argued a couple of years before she had come to work for the firm, the result of which had been Edward cutting himself off from his family completely. The name Edward had never been mentioned among his family either, and any photographs of him that might once have been in the house had been long since removed when Juliet had arrived on the scene.

Not that any of that had mattered to Juliet; it was all family history, and, she being an orphan herself, family relationships were a bit of a mystery to her anyway. At the time she had been too much in love with Simon to care about anything else. And to her amazement that love had been returned, their romance being of the whirlwind type, the two of them spending all of their free time together. With the approval of William. He had seemed pleased that his son was settling down, had welcomed Juliet into his home and his warm affection.

It was the first taste of any real family that Juliet had ever had, and she remembered how she couldn't help wondering how 'my dear older brother', as Simon sardonically called him, could ever have distanced himself from that closeness.

But it had only been a fleeting thought, drawn as she had been into the lives of the Carlyle men, with William making her his personal secretary as her relationship with his son deepened.

And then had come the dreadful night that Simon had been killed. It was a night Juliet would never forget, the nightmare having remained with her for the last seven years. William, despite having now irrevocably lost his younger son, had been marvellous with her, the two of them forming a bond that night that was to last until the day William died.

It still existed as far as Juliet was concerned! But she knew that Liam Carlyle would never understand a bond like that, that he saw it only as black and white—mostly black! She had lived with his father in the family home, so therefore she must have been his father's mistress. How far from the truth he was! Juliet would never be any man's mistress. Nor any man's wife, for that matter. There had been no man in her life after Simon. And there never would be.

No man in that way anyway. But she seemed to be stuck with Liam in her life at the moment—a business partner for now—although she had a feeling that that might come to an end tomorrow morning.

She had tried. No one could say that she hadn't tried. But if she failed now she would still have let William down...

Sleep was even more impossible that night than it usually was. Juliet, finally having given up all pretence of even trying to sleep, got out of bed to go once again through the papers she had brought with her from England for Edward—Liam—Carlyle to look at.

It was all pretty straightforward really; she needed his signature on vital papers to be able to finance and maintain the company. Surely that wasn't going to be too much to ask? It wouldn't cost him anything, just his signature and a little of his time. But it was time which he had been refusing to let her have for the last two months...

She dressed carefully for her business meeting. Their encounters so far had been far from businesslike, and she had an idea that she was going to need all the confidence she had this morning!

Her skirt was neat, black, and tailored, finishing only slightly above her knee, the pale green blouse tucked in neatly at the narrow waist, her make-up minimal, her hair secured at her nape with a black slide. With her business file tucked under her arm she looked even more the part.

At least she hoped she did! The last thing she needed was to feel inadequate with Liam Carlyle.

The receptionist smiled at her enquiringly as she approached the desk.

Juliet returned the smile. 'I'm supposed to be meeting Mr Carlyle in one of the conference-rooms this morning.' It was more a statement than a query, but she had no idea which room Liam had chosen for their meeting.

'Miss Berkley?' the receptionist returned lightly.

Well, at least the young girl realised who she was, which was promising! 'That's right.' Juliet answered with some relief; she had had a terrible feeling, after the way she had left yesterday evening, that Liam might not even turn up.

'Miss Gilbraith is waiting for you in the coffee-lounge,' the receptionist informed her as she pointed in the direction of the elegantly furnished room to their left.

'Miss Gilbraith...?' Juliet frowned. Who on earth...?

'Mr Carlyle's assistant,' the young girl told her with another friendly smile.

Diana... But why was the other woman and not Liam waiting for her? Surely he hadn't decided to let his personal assistant deal with this? Did he really care so little for his father, or his father's business, that he had passed the responsibility for this on to someone else?

Juliet was barely aware of thanking the young girl behind the desk before she walked over to the lounge. She couldn't believe Liam had done this! Oh, she realised that there was still rancour inside him towards his father, but really, this was unbelievable!

Diana Gilbraith sat at a table near the window, looking uninterestedly out at the boats which were sailing in the bay. The other woman looked just as

chic as she had yesterday, today wearing a blue
sundress that showed off the depth of her tan and
made her hair appear blonder as it fell loosely to
her shoulders. If Juliet was dressed for business,
this other woman was dressed for a day in the sun!

Juliet straightened her shoulders as she approached the other woman, steeling her expression
to look confident and self-assured. 'Miss
Gilbraith?'

The other woman turned with a warm smile at
the query, standing up in one smooth, eye-catching
movement; if this woman was only Liam's personal assistant, Juliet would be very surprised!

'Miss Berkley,' she greeted warmly, the smile
reaching the deep blue of her eyes. 'And please call
me Diana.'

Juliet, given the circumstances, had been prepared to dislike the other woman—her defences
were already firmly in place—but now she found
it was impossible to resist her warmth. 'Juliet,' she
returned awkwardly. 'Is Mr Carlyle not with you?'
Obviously he wasn't, but how else was she to broach
the subject of Liam's whereabouts?

'Let's sit down, shall we?' Diana suggested
lightly, and waited until they were both seated
before resuming the conversation. 'Unfortunately
Liam had to leave early this morning,' she told
Juliet regretfully. 'But he asked me to make his
apologies.'

She just bet he had! 'Had to leave early this
morning' indeed. 'When will he be back?' she bit
out tightly, doing her damnedest to hide her disappointment and knowing that she must be failing

miserably; she had banked everything on this conversation with Liam, and now he wasn't even here!

'He didn't say.' Diana Gilbraith gave a vague shrug. 'But then, Liam is like that,' she added dismissively. 'He'll ring me when he needs me.'

Juliet could well imagine he would. Needed the other woman for what? she could have said, but somehow, despite the briefness of their acquaintance, she quite liked this woman sitting across from her, and felt, now that she had actually spoken to Diana, that she'd had no right to make the assumptions she had concerning her and her employer. Something about Diana Gilbraith said that they would be erroneous assumptions.

Of course, that could have something to do with the wedding-ring Diana wore on her left hand, Juliet acknowledged self-derisively. She had noticed the plain gold band, accompanied by a substantial solitaire diamond engagement ring, seconds ago.

But none of this helped Juliet; she needed to see Liam Carlyle, and he seemed to have disappeared off to goodness knew where, and even his personal assistant didn't know when he would be back!

She gave a heavy sigh. 'In that case there doesn't appear to be a lot more to say.' She grimaced, standing up. 'Thank you for at least letting me know,' she added politely; it was hardly Diana's fault that her employer had done a disappearing act.

'Oh, I don't think you quite understand.' Diana stopped her departure, giving a light, apologetic laugh. 'Maybe I haven't explained myself very well. Liam has gone to his villa in the hills; he would like you to join him there.'

Juliet stared down at the other woman, complete incomprehension in her expression, she was sure.

'I obviously haven't explained myself at all.' The other woman shook her head self-deprecatingly. 'You'll have to forgive me, Juliet; Liam has given me a week's holiday, starting today, and I'm quite excited at the prospect of going home to my family. But that's no reason for me to be burbling in this way.' She gave a rueful grimace. 'Liam wants you to drive down to his villa and——'

'Drive?' Juliet repeated dazedly, dropping back into her chair, still stunned by the knowledge that Liam had a villa on the island. She was even more stunned by the fact that he expected her to drive there; she had never driven on the right-hand side of the road before!

Diana nodded. 'There's a hire-car waiting outside for you. I'm to give you directions, and a map, of course, so that you don't get lost.'

Juliet was still having a problem taking all this in. Liam wanted her to drive to his villa somewhere on the island, and would talk business with her there? Why not here? Why did she have to go to his villa? Suddenly she knew exactly why: Liam Carlyle didn't like being told what to do, and last night she had dictated the time and place they were to meet!

It appeared that she had no choice but to make that drive.

'...and your account dealt with.' Diana Gilbraith was talking to her smilingly.

Juliet gave a dazed shake of her head. 'Sorry?' She had been so lost in her own thoughts that she hadn't heard a word the other woman had said.

'It's all right.' Diana smiled at her again. 'The island has that effect after a few days,' she excused. 'I always become very lethargic when we stay here. I was telling you that Liam has booked you out of the hotel and dealt with your account.'

Juliet blinked, stunned; she wasn't keeping up with this conversation at all! 'Why?' she frowned. But she had a feeling she already knew!

'You'll be staying at his villa now, of course,' Diana said dismissively, seeming to have no idea what effect this information was having on Juliet.

And it *was* having an effect! Liam had booked her out of the hotel, paid her account—an account which she had to admit she had been dreading receiving!—and now expected her to go and stay with him at his villa God knew where. And Liam, of course—but then, considering the autocratic way he was behaving, perhaps he thought he *was* God!

Or, more to the point, he knew he was the one with the power to dictate the terms and conditions of any further meetings between the two of them...

CHAPTER THREE

IF JULIET had been in the right frame of mind to enjoy it, the drive down the west coast of the island to Liam's villa would have been very pleasant; the views were magnificent. But she needed extreme concentration to make the drive at all, unaccustomed as she was to driving on the right-hand side of the road, and her thoughts were far from trouble-free too.

She felt like a puppet having its strings pulled—by Liam Carlyle. What could have been so important that he'd had to leave the hotel this morning before their meeting? Diana Gilbraith hadn't seemed to have the answer to that one—or if she had she wasn't telling. And the other woman had left too now, to go south and take a plane home to her family in England.

It was all very unexpected, and Juliet couldn't say she was exactly pleased at the thought of going to Liam's villa. She hadn't even realised, during all her effort to see him, that he had a villa on the island.

The man was as elusive as a chameleon!

And she had to try and do business with him. Try being the operative word; Juliet had a feeling that it was going to be more difficult than she had ever imagined. And she didn't at all like the feeling that she was being played with.

It seemed a long drive to Liam's villa, although in actual miles it probably wasn't that far. But she had no real idea of where she was going, and continually referred to the map Diana Gilbraith had given her, keeping a keen eye on the X that indicated where the actual villa was. It appeared to be just outside a village on the west coast of the island, and as she approached the village after lunch she kept an eye out for a sign that would indicate the villa, the name of which she couldn't have pronounced if she had tried to ask anyone.

Damn Liam Carlyle! She felt totally out of her depth—in a place she didn't know, a country whose language she couldn't understand, let alone speak!

She had actually driven through the village before she realised that she must have missed the villa completely. She had been so fascinated by the terraced village perched on the side of the hill, and the orange and lemon trees growing beside the houses on those terraces, that she had driven out the other side of the village before she knew what she was doing.

She was hot, tired and extremely irritable by the time she had reversed and driven back, finding the villa with no problem this time, although she was slightly put off by the rough track that seemed to lead down to it. Surely this couldn't be the right place? After the luxury she had just come from, this villa appeared to be rustic to say the least.

But the name appeared to be right, and even if it was the wrong villa perhaps the owner would be able to direct her to the right place.

If the owner had been at home! Several rings on the doorbell elicited no response, further increasing Juliet's irritability. Despite appearances this had to be the right place, she decided, and she had no intention of running all over the island looking for Liam. The damned man had booked her out of her hotel—OK, he had paid her bill in the process, but it was still a damned cheek!—and so she intended just camping out on his doorstep until he turned up!

If he turned up... There was always the possibility that he hadn't come here at all, that he literally had got her running all over the island for nothing. He——

'Come and have a swim; you look very hot and uncomfortable,' drawled an all too familiar voice.

Juliet spun round at once, colour warming her cheeks as she looked at Liam, standing at the side of the villa watching her, a towel secured about his waist, his torso completely bare, the dark blond hair there glistening in the sunshine. He looked tall and virile and slightly dangerous, like a predator about to pounce.

And she knew she looked hot and uncomfortable; she felt it too!

'I've been looking for this damned villa for almost an hour,' she exaggerated in her agitation. 'It's not exactly on the main road.' And that wasn't an exaggeration; she had driven almost half a mile down the track before the villa had even come into view!

'It's not meant to be,' Liam dismissed mockingly. 'It would hardly be a retreat if everyone could find it.'

She knew he had a point, but at the moment she was too disgruntled to admit it. 'Well, anyway, I'm here,' she snapped, eyes flashing.

'So I can see.' Liam's gaze moved over her slowly.

She looked a mess; she knew she did; the pale green sundress she had changed into for the drive was now creased and clinging to her in the heat of the afternoon sun; her hair, which she left secured, was once again escaping in silky tendrils about her face and neck. But if she looked a mess it was this man's fault. She was also hungry; she had eaten very little before leaving the hotel earlier, and hadn't stopped for lunch on the way here either. All in all, she was not in a good humour!

'We have some business to discuss,' she bit out tensely, aware that her head was starting to pound too, probably from the tension of the drive in the hot sunshine.

'Not until you've relaxed a bit—possibly had some lunch?' he added enquiringly. 'And then taken a swim to cool down.'

She knew her temper must show in her face, that the light sprinkling of freckles that dusted her nose would be showing in sharp contrast to the rest of her pale skin. Being a redhead, she didn't tan; her skin merely went red and then returned to its normal pallor. Her eyes were sparkling with temper, and her mouth seemed set in a firm, angry line.

Perhaps a swim wouldn't be a bad idea ... !

'I'll accept your last offer,' she snapped. 'Then we can discuss business. And then I'll have to organise a flight home.'

Liam put out a hand, indicating that she should precede him round to the back of the villa. The rustic, almost uncared for front of the villa in no way prepared Juliet for the back of it; there was a huge swimming-pool glistening in the sunshine, a beautiful flower-covered patio to one side, with loungers arranged amid the fragrant beauty, and a jug of iced fruit juice sitting on one of the tables. From the two glasses that sat next to the jug Juliet guessed that Liam had been expecting her any time now—or there was someone else in the villa with him.

'Help yourself.' He indicated the fruit juice. 'I would offer to get it for you, but the mood you're in you're likely to refuse it!' he added in an amused voice.

She was behaving childishly, she knew that, and it didn't help that he was pointing it out to her, but she did hate this feeling of being manipulated. It wasn't a feeling that sat well on her shoulders at all.

But to have refused the juice would have been pure madness on her part, considering how hot it was and just how thirsty she was too after her journey.

She gratefully sat down on one of the loungers, poured two glasses of juice, one for Liam and one for herself, and drank thirstily. It was delicious, and seemed to be a combination of orange and grapefruit juice.

'Better?' Liam sat down next to her, sipping at his own juice as he looked at her with mocking blue eyes.

'Much,' she nodded, looking about her appreciatively at the panoramic views down to the deep blue sea.

'Does this "damned villa" meet with your approval?' he drawled.

She turned sharply back to him. 'It's very nice,' she bit out tautly.

'I think so,' he nodded, relaxing back on the lounger, the towel shifting to reveal the considerable length of his muscular legs.

Juliet looked away, feeling uncomfortable again—this time because of the presence of this half-naked man. Although Liam seemed completely unconcerned with his lack of clothing. And why shouldn't he be? This was his home, his 'retreat'; he could walk around completely naked if he chose to, although she was relieved that he wasn't!

She did, however, have a slight puzzle over why he should have invited her here to his obviously very private domain in the first place; it was obviously a very private place of his, had none of the overwhelming luxury of the hotel she had just left, and seemed to be somewhere where he came to relax completely, away from all his business pressures.

And she did feel very alone with him here, apparently several miles away from other habitation...

He sat up suddenly, and Juliet made an involuntary movement backwards. Liam frowned across at her. 'I was just going to suggest that we go for that swim now that you've cooled down a little...' He studied her intently, eyes narrowed thoughtfully.

She swallowed hard, realising that she was behaving like some gauche teenager rather than the twenty-seven-year-old businesswoman she wanted Liam to think her. She just wasn't used to being around partially clothed men, under any circumstances . . .

She nodded abruptly. 'I'll go and get my costume from the car.'

'Does that mean I have to put one on too?' Liam said softly.

Her eyes widened; he wasn't wearing anything under that towel! Oh, God . . . ! 'I think that might be best,' she told him tightly as she stood up. 'In the circumstances.'

'And what circumstances might those be?' Liam stood up too, dangerously close to her. 'The fact that you were my father's mistress?' he added scathingly.

Juliet gasped at this unexpected attack. 'I——'

'Because you're completely safe with me, Juliet,' he rasped harshly. '*In the circumstances*!'

'I was not your father's mistress!' she protested incredulously.

'Weren't you?' He turned away disgustedly to enter the villa through the huge open glass sliding doors.

Juliet stared after him, too stunned to move, blinking back the tears that had suddenly blinded her. It had never occurred to her, or, she was sure, to William either, that such an assumption could be made about their relationship. By anyone. William had been the father she had never known, especially after Simon's death, and it was unthinkable that Liam should now make such an accusation.

But he *had* made it. Obviously believed it. And, with William dead, she had no way of proving otherwise.

And why should she? Liam made no secret of the fact that he felt nothing but contempt for his father—a man she had loved, and who, she was sure, had loved her in return. She owed Liam no explanations about a father whose funeral he hadn't even bothered to attend.

Once she had got over William's sudden death from a heart attack, she had informed Liam's London office of his father's funeral, and had been stunned when he hadn't even turned up for that.

The wording of William's will made it obvious that he had wanted to heal the rift between himself and his son—even if only after his death—which was why she had felt honour-bound at least to contact Edward Carlyle and tell him of the arrangements. The fact that he hadn't come had told her that he didn't have the same wish to heal the rift. It was only when it had become obvious that she couldn't run the business without his co-operation that she had decided to contact him again.

And how she wished she hadn't had to; she hated the way he spoke about William so scathingly.

She was still sitting on the lounger when Liam came back out of the villa a few minutes later, wearing dark blue swimming-trunks now. His body was lean and fit and deeply tanned, and his hair had dried to a deep gold.

'Changed your mind about the swim?' he derided, poised on the edge of the pool.

She had changed her mind about everything concerning him. She should have known what sort of man he was when he hadn't returned for William's funeral, when he'd continued to ignore all her letters and telephone calls. She was wasting her time even trying to talk to him, was putting herself through unnecessary humiliation when it was obvious that he had no real intention of talking to her about Carlyle Properties. He never had had.

'I have to go,' she told him abruptly, standing up. 'This was a mistake.'

Liam arched dark blond brows. 'Any more of a mistake than flying out here in the first place?' he bit out scathingly.

He was right; it had been a mistake, Liam had no intention of being co-operative over his father's company.

'It appears not,' she accepted contemptuously. 'I would have thought you owed your father——'

'I owe William Carlyle nothing!' he cut in forcefully, a nerve pulsing in his cheek as he glared across at her, his eyes glittering fiercely. 'He only had one son—Simon. Did he never tell you that?' he scorned.

Juliet blinked across at him. It had been so long since anyone had mentioned Simon. She and William, by tacit agreement, had never talked about him; the memories were too painfully deep. And now Liam was opening up a wound that had never really had the chance to heal . . . !

She moistened suddenly dry lips. 'Simon is dead.' Her voice broke huskily.

'And so was I, for over ten years. William can't just suddenly claim our relationship now that he's dead!' Liam snarled angrily. 'William Carlyle had no sons when he died, Juliet,' he rasped viciously. 'So how could he possibly have left half his

company to one of them? Take the company,
Juliet—I think you probably earned it!'

With that last contemptuous statement he dived
smoothly into the water beneath him, surfacing
seconds later to swim the length of the pool with
smooth, strong strokes.

She wanted to leave—had to leave—but somehow
she couldn't move; her legs felt like lead weights.

There had been a lot of bitterness behind Liam's
words about his father, and bitterness, as she very
well knew, was based on pain, a pain that went so
deep that bitterness was needed to survive it. She
had no idea what William and Liam had argued
about all those years ago—William had never talked
about his elder son—but she did know Liam had
never really got over the pain of walking out on
the only family he had.

Ten years. It was a long time not to have recognised your family. As far as Juliet was aware Liam
seemed to have no ties now either; he seemed to go
wherever he wanted. What he seemed to have spent
his time doing during the last ten years was building
himself a business empire in the world of hotels
and leisure, becoming more successful in that field
than his father's business could ever hope to be.
Perhaps as a way of hitting out at his father? Juliet
was no psychologist, but that was more than
a possibility.

And it seemed that he had now finished hitting
out at her for her involvement with his father, that
the game was now over and she could have Carlyle
Properties as far as he was concerned!

She didn't doubt for one moment that Liam
meant what he said; she was sure that he was a man

who always meant what he said. But how could she take something which she knew she had no right to? *Her* initial reaction on being told that she owned half the company had been to give Edward Carlyle all of it; after all, she had no real right to it. But his elusiveness over the last two months had shown her only too clearly just how interested he was in the company.

Even so, she couldn't just walk away with all of the company. That would be so totally wrong. And it obviously wasn't what William had wanted at all.

'Still here?' Liam rasped as he swung easily out of the pool, picking up a towel to begin towelling himself dry. 'You've got what you came for, Juliet,' he derided. 'We have nothing further to discuss.'

Her eyes flashed a warning. He might have been hurt by William in the past, might now have reason to believe that she had been his father's mistress, but that did not give him the right to talk to her in that way!

'There will be papers to sign——'

'Send them to my London office.' He waved a hand in dismissal. 'My lawyers will deal with them.'

'But——'

'Juliet,' he cut in quietly—too quietly, 'haven't you realised by now that I have no interest in anything to do with the Carlyle family?' His eyes glittered deeply blue.

'Your name is Carlyle——'

'For my sins,' he accepted abruptly, the towel draped about his neck now. 'But a name doesn't make me one of them.'

She frowned across at him. He spoke of his father and brother with real hatred, a hatred that went very deep...

'Don't look so shocked, Juliet,' he said derisively. 'Not everyone can love the family they're given.'

She stiffened. 'I wouldn't know about that,' she bit out.

He looked at her blankly for a moment, and then winced as he realised exactly what she meant. 'Oh. God, I'm sorry.' He shook his head.

Having a family of her own had been something she had longed for when she had been younger, but for some reason the mother she had never seen had refused to let her be put up for adoption, and the series of foster homes she had gone to had all become just a blur of kind, well-meaning people who could never really allow themselves to become too attached to her, or her to them. And then her mother had died when she was fifteen. At that age Juliet had been far too old to be wanted for adoption, and had left foster care, as soon as she was old enough, to make a life for herself.

That was why William's kindness to her, both before and after Simon's death, had been so important to her; why she felt such an obligation, despite Liam's insults concerning her relationship with his father, to try and reach his older son now.

'It isn't important,' she dismissed.

'Yes, it is, damn it,' Liam rasped. 'Look, let's have some lunch, Juliet, and then maybe both of us will have calmed down slightly.'

As far as she was aware, she wasn't upset, but if Liam chose to see it that way that was up to him.

And she really did need one more chance to change
his mind about Carlyle Properties.

'I won't change my mind about any involvement
with my father's company.' He seemed to read her
mind as they went into the house to prepare lunch.
'I cut myself off from that once, and I intend to
remain away from it!'

'Liam . . .'

'Juliet . . .' he returned mockingly, his ill humour
from a few minutes ago definitely abating. 'Don't
try and interfere in things you don't understand,'
he advised quietly.

'But——'

'Lunch,' he announced firmly as they entered the
kitchen—a bright open room, its general clutter
fitting the rustic image.

Liam went to the fridge and began to take out
salad stuff and cold meats and cheeses. This obviously really was his retreat from the outside world,
a place where he was completely alone. Usually.
But unfortunately, Juliet knew, her presence here
meant nothing; Liam really was adamant about
Carlyle Properties.

They worked together in silence preparing the
meal, taking their laden plates back outside to sit
beside the pool and eat the food.

'And I expect you to eat that,' Liam warned as
she picked at the food on her plate. 'By the look
of you, someone should have taken you in hand
years ago!' He ate his own food with obvious
enjoyment.

Juliet looked at him impatiently. 'Not only are
you thoughtless, you're arrogant too!'

He grinned at her unconcernedly. 'It has been said,' he acknowledged with a nod.

A man in his position could probably afford to be arrogant, but Juliet found it more than a little unnerving being ordered about in this way. She and William had always worked as a team and since his death she had been the one giving orders, to household and company staff alike.

'The house,' she said abruptly. 'What do you want me to do with that?'

Liam's eyes narrowed. 'As far as I'm aware that was left to you,' he dismissed harshly.

So he *had* read the letters sent to him by the lawyers, and probably hers too, even if he had chosen to ignore them! Which proved that he wasn't quite as unconcerned about his father as he liked to appear.

She shrugged. 'It's your family home——' She broke off as she saw the darkening anger on his face. 'It's called Carlyle House, Liam,' she reasoned.

'Then change its name. Or your own,' he rasped. 'It's something I should have done myself years ago!'

'I——'

'Wine.' He stood up abruptly. 'We should have some wine with this,' he announced before striding back into the villa.

Juliet stared after him. He really was the most difficult man to understand. In fact, she wasn't even bothering to try any more! One minute he was civil and the next he was on the attack again. Admittedly, the attacks only came when the conversation veered on to his family, but considering that was all they really had to talk about it was a strain, to say the least!

She wordlessly took the glass of wine he handed her a few minutes later, sipping gratefully at the golden liquid.

'Eat,' he instructed harshly.

She looked at him over the rim of her wine glass. 'Liam——'

'Just eat, Juliet,' he said impatiently. 'I didn't ask for you to come to Majorca, to seek me out—and too much of that wine on an empty stomach and I'm likely to have a drunken woman on my hands!'

He really was the most insulting man! She had never been drunk in her life, rarely touched alcohol, in fact, and Liam certainly had no right to imply that she was going to get drunk on one glass of wine.

Thoughtless. Difficult. Arrogant. Insulting. He had been all four of those already this afternoon, was there anything nice to say about this man?

She didn't look at him again as she ate some of the food, defiantly taking sips of the wine in between eating, realising after a while, and two refills of her glass of wine later, that she was actually starting to feel a little light-headed. The long drive on unfamiliar roads, too much heat and sun, followed by the tension of trying to talk to Liam, she excused herself. It certainly had nothing to do with the wine!

'How long have you owned this villa?' She decided to try polite conversation again.

'Long enough,' Liam returned tersely.

So much for polite conversation! Why bother? she asked herself dismissively.

'I only asked,' she muttered, taking another sip of the wine.

'And I only answered,' he returned abruptly.

'Not exactly,' she challenged.

'How "exactly" did you want me to answer?' he derided. 'Do you just want a year-month approximation of how long I've owned the villa, or do you want to know to the day?'

'Oh, just forget it,' Juliet snapped. 'It wasn't important anyway.'

'Then why ask?' he said scornfully.

'I thought one of us should try to be polite,' she returned scathingly. 'Obviously only one of us is capable of it!'

Liam shrugged unconcernedly. 'Obviously only one of us needs to be.'

Juliet drew in an angry breath; he was insulting to the point of rudeness! He didn't know her, didn't really know anything about her—except what he chose to make up in his more than fertile mind!— and he had no right to speak to her like this.

'I've had enough.' She put her plate, most of the food still on it, back on the table with her empty wine glass next to it. This had been a waste of her time, as well as his!

'I think we both have,' he acknowledged grimly. 'You've brought something back into my life that I would rather forget about, Juliet,' he bit out.

She looked at him with wide accusing eyes. 'You can't forget about your own father!'

'Why not?' His eyes glittered, deeply blue. 'He forgot about me for ten years!'

'William is dead, Liam,' she said in exasperation, tears in her eyes now as she thought of the loss of the man who had cared for her so much. 'Dead!' she repeated forcefully. 'You can't retain bitterness towards someone who's dead!'

He shook his head. 'I stopped feeling bitterness towards him a long time ago. In fact, I stopped feeling anything towards him a long time ago!' he added harshly.

Juliet stared at him for several long, seemingly timeless minutes, unable to reconcile inside herself the feelings Liam had for a man who had shown her nothing but tender kindness. And no matter what Liam said he did show bitterness towards his father. She knew that emotion only too well herself not to recognise it, but she had never felt it towards William.

'I think I had better go,' she finally said quietly, standing up.

Liam looked up at her, squinting in the bright sunshine. 'You haven't booked your flight yet,' he pointed out softly.

And now that she had stood up she wasn't sure she was capable of doing so, or of driving down to Palma; her head had started to spin, unaccustomed to wine with little food. God, the last thing she wanted to do, after bristling so indignantly at the suggestion that she might get drunk, was let Liam know that she really didn't feel too well!

She shook her head, trying to think clearly. 'I can do that when I get to Palma,' she parried, just wanting to get away from here now before Liam realised the truth—that he had 'a drunken woman on his hands'!

She wasn't exactly drunk, she reassured herself; she just didn't feel quite as capable as she usually did. In fact, she felt incapable of moving at this moment.

Liam stood up next to her, and looked down at her intently. 'Are you all right?' He frowned. 'You've gone very pale.'

She knew she had; she had felt the colour draining from her face even as he had said the words. And the sun reflecting off the blue of the swimming-pool was starting to make her feel dizzy, although at the same time she felt mesmerised by the flickering light, unable to look away.

'Juliet?' Liam prompted again, sharply this time.

She looked up at him finally, blinking rapidly as she tried to focus. Liam's face was just a hazy outline, and the more she blinked, the more unfocused it became.

Liam grasped her by her upper arms as she swayed slightly. 'Juliet, what——?'

Juliet didn't hear any more; blackness washed over her as she felt herself falling, falling, falling...

CHAPTER FOUR

'WELL, I can honestly say that's the first time a woman has fallen for me in quite that way,' drawled the voice that was becoming all too familiar.

Juliet opened one eyelid—it was about all she could manage to do at this precise moment. Her whole body, including her eyelids, felt like a lead weight. And the sun blazing into the room made her close even that eyelid as its brightness dazzled her.

'Wakey, wakey,' Liam encouraged—far too boisterously as far as she was concerned. 'Come on, Juliet, drink some of this juice; you'll feel better for it.'

At this moment she didn't think she would ever feel better again. If this was what it felt like to drink too much she knew why it had never happened to her before! Her head was thumping, her body ached, and her mouth felt as if it had fur growing in it. And people actually drank alcohol on a social basis as a way of enjoying themselves; they must all be masochists, she decided.

'Juliet, it's time to wake up,' Liam encouraged in that cheerful, over-loud voice.

Why was it? she wanted to know. She just wanted to go back to sleep until she felt human again. If she ever did!

'What was that?' Liam prompted jovially as she mumbled under her breath.

'I said——' She winced even at the sound of her own voice. 'I said,' she said again, much more quietly this time, 'stop talking in that loud voice. And it's much too bright in here.'

'I'm talking perfectly normally,' he informed her lightly, although his voice did seem to be slightly softer. 'And I'll draw the curtains if that will make you feel better.'

Curtains? What curtains? Where...? Juliet opened both her eyes in time to see Liam walk across the room, feeling sudden panic as she realised that she was in a bedroom, actually lying in the bed! In the bed? What...?

'There.' Liam had turned back to her, dressed now in a dark blue shirt and light-coloured denims. 'How are you feeling this morning?'

Morning? What...?

'Dear, dear, dear, Juliet,' Liam drawled as he walked over to stand beside her. 'You are in a sorry state, aren't you?' He shook his head mockingly as he sat down on the side of the bed. 'You've been asleep for about sixteen hours and you still can't think straight, can you?'

Sixteen hours! Then she hadn't misheard; it *was* morning!

She went to sit up—only to find herself trapped beneath the bedclothes because of Liam sitting on the bed in the way that he was. She swallowed hard. 'How did I get here?' Her mouth still felt as if it was full of cotton wool and her voice was husky.

Liam folded his arms across his chest. 'How do you think you got here?' he taunted. 'I didn't drag you here by your hair, if that's what you think.'

Her scalp tingled enough for that to have actually been a possibility! But no, Liam must have carried her here. He must have put her to bed too.

She swallowed hard. 'I can't think what happened...'

'Can't you?' He looked down at her with a too innocent expression.

Juliet wished he would stop looking so damned cheerful! She had made a complete fool of herself and he was obviously enjoying the fact. That wasn't very gentlemanly. But then, when had Liam ever been a gentleman where she was concerned? The one and only time she could remember was when he had stood up as she had got to the table in the hotel restaurant the very first night they met.

God, that was only two days ago! She felt as if he had always been in her life, tormenting her.

She attempted to moisten her lips, but there was no moisture on her tongue to do so. 'I must have got a slight touch of sunstroke,' she excused, avoiding his gaze as she sat up slightly to take a drink of the juice he had put on the bedside table for her.

'Or something,' Liam drawled derisively. 'I hate to tell you this, Juliet, but the sun isn't hot enough in Majorca in November to give you sunstroke.'

Juliet barely heard his reply, horrified to have realised as she sat up that she was wearing nothing but her bra and pants beneath the bedclothes. Liam had undressed her before putting her to bed!

'You've gone very pale again.' His voice sharpened almost accusingly. And Juliet quickly realised why. 'You aren't pregnant, are you?' he added harshly.

She gave an involuntary gasp. 'Of course I'm not pregnant,' she protested, holding the bedclothes to her protectively now.

'I don't see why there's any "of course not" about it,' he dismissed scornfully. 'You've been living with my father for seven years!'

'I told you——' She broke off, the rise in her voice causing her head to thump again. She closed her eyes, willing herself to calm down; Liam seemed to enjoy getting a reaction out of her where his father was concerned, and she wasn't about to give him that satisfaction just now. 'I'm not pregnant,' she repeated flatly.

How could she possibly be pregnant, when there had been no one in her life since Simon? Liam could think what he liked about his father—nothing she said seemed to convince him otherwise—but she knew the truth. And there was no way she could possibly be pregnant. By anyone.

'You're as white as the sheets.' Liam's voice was still accusing.

'I'll be fine once I've showered and dressed,' she told him defensively, unwilling to tell him just how awful she really felt—or to let him know just how desperately she wanted him to leave so that she could put some clothes on.

He looked down at her, his expression sceptical. 'Somehow I doubt it,' he finally drawled.

'Look, I'm sorry if I've inconvenienced you by apparently passing out in this way,' she snapped waspishly. 'The wine may have—all right, *did* go to my head,' she corrected herself impatiently at his derisive expression. 'But I'll be on my way and out of your hair——'

'Out of my bed,' he corrected her. 'I own the villa,' he reminded her softly as she frowned.

She looked up at him sharply, relieved that it wasn't actually *his* bed but at the same time totally disconcerted by the way he was looking at her. His gaze softened, a smile playing about his lips.

There was a sudden tension in the room. Their gazes locked, grey clashing with dark blue. Juliet was suddenly very aware of Liam's closeness to her on the side of the bed, the warm heat emanating from his body, the slightly discernible smell of his aftershave. And of her own barely clothed body...

The bedclothes were still pulled up to her chin, but her shoulders and arms were bare, her hair a mass of tumbled red curls against her heated flesh. And this man had undressed her last night, had seen her wearing only the cream bra and panties.

She had never really thought about her body, about whether or not she was attractive to men, having no interest in them herself, but now, surprisingly, she wondered what Liam had thought of her long, silken limbs, of the slight swell of her breasts, the smooth curve of her hips and thighs...

God, not only was she suddenly completely aware of her own body but she was aware of the muscled strength of Liam's too. His shirt was partially unbuttoned to reveal the golden hair that grew against the tanned skin there. She had never felt so physically aware of a man before. And it wasn't something she wanted to feel now, either—not at all, but especially not for this man.

'If you'll go I'll just shower and dress and then leave,' she said stiltedly, her gaze remaining unblinkingly on the harsh attraction of his face.

His mouth curved into a smile, revealing even white teeth, deep grooves beside that mouth testifying to the fact that he smiled often. Normally. When not in the company of a woman he thought had been his father's mistress!

'There's no hurry,' he said huskily, reaching out to pick up a curling strand of her hair, his fingers lightly brushing the bareness of her shoulder as he did so. 'Is there?' he added softly.

Juliet swallowed hard, unable to stop the involuntary shiver that ran down her spine even at that light touch from the slender but powerful-looking hand. 'I think we've agreed that we have nothing else to talk about,' she said breathlessly.

'Have we?' Liam was suddenly much closer, his face only inches away from hers now, and Juliet was able to see the darker flecks of colour in the blue of his eyes, the golden length of his lashes. 'Perhaps we could find something else,' he murmured throatily.

She couldn't imagine what. And she wished he would stop playing with her hair like that. Several curls wound about the length of his fingers now— fingers that kept lightly brushing against her bare shoulder.

'I don't think so.' She was pressed right back into the pillow now as she shook her head, keeping herself as far away from Liam as possible given the fact that she was lying in the bed while he sat beside and over her. 'It was a mistake coming here.'

'I've never brought a woman here before,' he mused softly, that darkened gaze roaming slowly over her now flushed features.

She thought that was the whole point; *he* hadn't brought her here now, and he resented the fact that she had intruded on his life in this way, considering her connection to his father—a connection that brought back memories he would rather forget.

But at the same time she found it difficult to believe that he had never brought a girlfriend or mistress to this remote villa; it was the perfect place to come for privacy and relaxation.

'You didn't bring one here this time, either,' she said. 'I came here to talk about your father,' she deliberately reminded him, knowing she had to put an end to this intimacy as soon as possible. It was far, far too dangerous.

The mention of his father acted like a slap in the face to Liam, who sat back sharply, untangling his hand from her hair before rising abruptly to his feet. 'So you did,' he acknowledged harshly. 'I'll go and get some coffee on. Come through when you're ready.' He strode purposefully from the room, closing the door forcefully behind him.

Juliet felt herself start to breathe again, deep, controlling breaths, and it took her several minutes to calm down her jangled nerves. Even so, she was still shaking slightly. And she didn't think that it had anything to do with the wine consumption of yesterday!

What had Liam been doing? She hadn't been mistaken about the desire she had seen in his eyes; she was sure she hadn't. And, from a man who had shown her nothing but contempt since acknowledging that he knew exactly who she was, she found that more than a little disturbing. Had he been intent on seducing her himself, just to prove that everything he had accused her of was true? It seemed the most logical explanation, and it was one that Juliet viewed with horror. There had been no possibility of her responding to that seduction, but even so it wasn't pleasant to realise just what contempt Liam held her in.

She threw back the bedclothes, swinging her legs to the floor to stand up and walk through to what she could see was an adjoining bathroom. At least, she would have walked through to that room if her legs hadn't given way the moment she stood up. Juliet felt herself falling and, unable to stop herself, knocked against the bedside table as she did so. The empty glass that had contained the juice fell too, smashing beside her on the cool marble floor.

She sat dazed on the ground for several seconds, unable to take in properly what had happened. Surely this couldn't still be the effect of the wine?

'What the hell...!' Liam burst back into the room, frowning darkly as he reached her side.

'Mind the glass!' she warned, too late, as he began to swear after stepping on a piece of the glass with his bare feet.

'Never mind that,' he dismissed, brushing the glass, which hadn't penetrated the skin, off his foot. 'What happened?' He came down on his haunches beside her.

She swallowed hard, pushing back the heavy swath of her hair. 'I'm not sure. One minute I was standing up, the next I had—well, I fell over,' she finished lamely, wishing once again that she had more clothes on than her brief underwear; she had never worn so little in a man's company before. And Liam Carlyle of all people!

His eyes narrowed to steely slits as his gaze ran over the slender length of her body. 'Are you sure you aren't pregnant?' he finally bit out.

Juliet drew in a sharp breath, her cheeks flushed, her mouth a thin, angry line. 'I told you, no!' she snapped forcefully, meeting his gaze challengingly.

Liam met that gaze for several seconds, then he shook his head. 'Then what the hell is wrong with you?' he rasped. 'Because this isn't a normal reaction to an excess of alcohol.'

'I didn't drink that much——'

'I don't really think that's relevant any more, Juliet,' he calmly interrupted her angry protest.

'Then why do you keep mentioning it?' Her eyes flashed, deeply grey.

'I think you should see a doctor,' he said thoughtfully, ignoring her outburst.

'Don't be ridiculous,' Juliet scorned, holding on to the bed as she got slowly to her feet. The world wasn't spinning quite so much now. If she just took things slowly...

'Get back into bed,' Liam ordered as he straightened. 'I'm going to call a friend of mine who's a doctor.'

'I don't want to see a doctor,' she insisted stubbornly—but she got back into the bed none the less, her legs starting to shake once again.

'I don't recall asking you what you wanted,' Liam told her arrogantly. 'You're a guest in my home, you obviously aren't well, so you'll see a doctor.'

So there! God, he was the most bossy man! 'I don't have any say in this at all?' she challenged.

'None whatsoever,' he confirmed flatly.

'You don't want a corpse on your hands!' she said derisively.

He looked down at her coldly. 'A corpse would be more difficult to deal with than a sick woman,' he announced before once again leaving the bedroom.

Juliet's mouth set mutinously as she sat up in the bed. She was convinced that whatever was wrong with her it was nothing serious. And she still intended leaving here—as soon as she could stand up long enough to get dressed!

'Exhaustion!' Liam said disgustedly, once again sitting on the side of Juliet's bed, which was in the guest bedroom, she had discovered once the doctor had arrived.

Liam's friend Tomás had been very friendly and nice but extremely thorough in his medical examination of her, finally announcing that she was obviously suffering from exhaustion, and that she didn't eat regularly, or often enough, to sustain her busy life. The last point Juliet could really have done without, given Liam's remarks already about her eating habits.

'What the hell have you been doing to get exhausted?' Liam demanded now, his gaze narrowed on her pale face. 'I thought you had been on holiday for the last week,' he added accusingly.

Juliet saw red at his attitude. What had she been doing? 'I've been trying to run a company for the last two months with a partner who refuses to be co-operative!' She glared up at him.

'So it's my fault, is it?' he said scathingly.

'Not completely,' she accepted, knowing it hadn't just been the last two months that had been so fraught with tension and hard work; that she had been working long and hard for Carlyle Properties for a long, long time. But it had filled her life, kept her busy, hadn't allowed her time to think or brood on other things.

'But your attitude certainly hasn't helped.' She wasn't about to let him off that easily; the last two months of just trying to speak to him had been absolute hell. 'And as for being on holiday this last week . . .' she gave him a pitying look '. . . we both know that isn't true.'

He stood up abruptly. 'So you are saying that this is my fault because I've been difficult about Carlyle Properties?' He walked over to the window, staring out down the valley to the clear blue sea.

Juliet looked at the rigidity of the broadness of his back. She could say that the strain of the last couple of months had nothing to do with the way she felt now, but it would be a lie; the last two months had been a nightmare as far as she personally was concerned.

'I said it hasn't helped,' she said again quietly.

Liam turned abruptly to face her. 'I need to think about this.' He strode over to the door. 'I'll bring you some lunch in a short while.'

'Er—could I have my suitcase from the car?' Juliet asked almost timidly, sensing that Liam was very close to exploding—he wasn't a man who liked to be made aware of his shortcomings. 'I would like to get dressed in some clean clothes before I leave,' she explained, at his frowning look.

His mouth thinned. 'I'll get your suitcase, Juliet, so that you can put a nightgown on or something, and be more comfortable in bed. But you aren't leaving just yet,' he added grimly.

Her eyes widened. 'But——'

'Nothing is going to change concerning Carlyle Properties in the next twenty-four hours or so. And Tomás said you needed to rest, and improve your diet,' he rasped uncompromisingly. 'And I told you, I need to think.'

And she could damn well do what she was told while he thought! Really, the man was impossible. But if at the end of that thinking he decided to be more helpful where the company was concerned maybe this one extra day would be worth the wait. Although she couldn't give it any longer than that, as she needed to get back.

'I don't need to stay in bed.'

'Tomás said you were to rest, and rest is what you will damn well do!' Liam bit out challengingly.

Juliet had never met a man like this one before. He was certainly nothing like William, who had been very gentlemanly and caring, welcoming her opinion on things, treating her as his equal. Liam just treated her like a rather wearing complication in his life. Which she supposed she was.

'Just the suitcase, then,' she accepted—although if he thought she was staying here any longer than the stated twenty-four hours he was in for a disappointment; she simply didn't have the time to waste lying around in bed doing nothing!

He nodded abruptly before leaving, but Juliet had no sooner sunk back on the pillows with a weary sigh than he was back again, with the suitcase, which he deposited just inside the bedroom, giving her a glaring look before leaving again.

And a good day to you too, Juliet thought ruefully as she got out of the bed to find some fresh clothes in her suitcase. She realised that she was a nuisance to him, that he didn't want her here, but *he* was the one insisting that she had to stay!

Men! No... she slowly corrected herself. Just Liam Carlyle. He had been alternately challenging her and taunting her since the moment she had first met him—except for those few brief minutes when she had thought he wanted something else from her. But she didn't want to think about them, didn't want to admit that, for a very short time, she had been extremely aware of him as the attractive man he undoubtedly was. As he had seemed aware of her.

But that was no good; he was William's son, and, more to the point, he was Simon's brother...!

'Now eat,' Liam instructed tersely, having allowed her to get up and join him for lunch beside the pool when she had refused to have the meal on a tray in bed. 'I don't know what my father has been doing with you, but you look as if you would snap in half if any more pressure were put on you!' he added disgustedly.

'I told you——' Juliet kept her own temper with effort '—William didn't do anything with me.'

'Just kept a fatherly eye on you, did he?' Liam sneered. 'Well, he did a damn awful job of it!'

She had been trying to eat some of the fruit, cheeses and fresh bread that Liam had provided for lunch, but it seemed that every time she even attempted to eat in this man's company he started an argument. They were never going to agree over their opinion concerning William, and so to talk about the older man at all was futile.

'Why are you selling your hotel complex over here?' She attempted to change the subject.

Dark blond brows rose over cool blue eyes. 'Who says I am?'

Juliet frowned. 'Your secretary——' She broke off, looking at him closely, finally putting down the orange she had been attempting to eat. 'Did you enjoy playing your little game with me, Liam?' she said sharply, suddenly knowing that that was exactly what he had been doing, realising too late that no secretary of Liam's would have been so indiscreet as to reveal such privileged information concerning his whereabouts, and the apparent sale of one of his hotels, to a complete stranger over the telephone. Unless she had been meant to!

The pig! The absolute lousy, rotten, manipulative——

'Not particularly.' He shook his head. 'Certainly not once I had met you,' he added grimly. 'You aren't what I expected, Juliet.' His eyes were narrowed on her thoughtfully, as if part of him still wasn't sure exactly what she was, just that she wasn't what he had 'expected'!

She could imagine only too well what he *had* expected and it wasn't very pleasant. Oh, she realised that, on the face of it, it didn't look too good in her favour: she was a young woman who had apparently been living with a much older man for several years. But it had been something which she was sure that William had never actually thought about, and she certainly hadn't—not until Liam's obviously cutting remarks about the relationship had forced her to do so.

'And considering the state of you my father obviously got his pound of flesh out of you,' Liam added harshly.

Juliet gasped—something she seemed to do all too often around this man. But he made such outrageous remarks it was impossible not to!

'Work-wise, I meant, of course,' he added scornfully.

'Of course,' she acknowledged bitingly.

'I thought I told you to eat.' He looked down pointedly at the food still on her plate.

'And you're used to people doing what you tell them to, aren't you?' Juliet derided.

'Usually, yes,' he said without conceit. 'I run a multi-million-pound corporation, Juliet; someone has to give the orders.'

And a little company like Carlyle Properties wasn't even worth the trouble of thinking about, she could see that. Except that it had been his father's company. But William had been a father he obviously despised, for some reason.

'I'm not one of your employees, Liam,' she told him calmly. 'And arguing like this when I'm trying to eat does not help my appetite!'

He gave a grimace. 'So I'm to blame for that too, am I?' He shook his head ruefully. 'I bet you're formidable in business, aren't you? No one would believe there's a woman of steel under that fragile-looking exterior!'

'Woman of steel'? He had to be joking! Oh, she had learnt to adopt a certain barrier to a lot of the knocks of life, but she certainly wouldn't call herself steely!

'Maybe I can understand why the old man kept you around, after all,' Liam mused. 'If all else failed, he brought in the big guns!'

'Liam——'

'Or, in this case, the little guns,' he continued derisively, pointedly looking her up and down. 'Who could possibly be a hard-headed businessman to a little runt like you?' He shook his head again.

He could, Juliet could have pointed out. But didn't. She was far too busy taking exception to the 'little runt' remark. 'Your father kept me on as his assistant because I was—am!—good at my job,' she told him stiltedly. 'For no other reason!'

Liam shrugged. 'But it's obviously proved too much for you since my father died.'

She drew in a ragged breath. Of course it had been too much for her since William died; she had been swimming upstream for the last two months— without any help from this man sitting beside her, she might add!

She sat very straight, her back rigid. 'Maybe if you had cared, just once, to come and actually look at Carlyle Properties you would have seen just how well it's run,' she bit out tautly.

Liam gave a considering nod. 'I intend to do just that.'

Juliet looked at him sharply, but his expression was enigmatic, his gaze steadily meeting hers. 'What do you mean?' she prompted warily.

He shrugged again. 'I've been giving the matter some thought and I've decided to come back to

England with you after all and take a look at the books of Carlyle Properties.'

Juliet stared at him. Just stared at him. Just exactly why had he changed his mind so suddenly?

CHAPTER FIVE

'GOOD God, nothing has changed!'

Juliet turned as she stood in the large reception area of Carlyle House, her brows raised, to look at Liam who was standing just behind her.

They had returned to England only that morning. On Liam's private jet. As she should have predicted! However Liam might have left this house, and his family, ten years ago, he certainly travelled and lived in style now, his jet of luxurious proportions, the formalities at the airport dealt with so quickly that Juliet had barely had time to catch her breath before going outside and being shown into the sporty Jaguar that Liam apparently liked to drive himself around England in.

He had unerringly driven both of them to Carlyle House this afternoon; he might not have visited the family home since he walked out all those years ago, but he certainly hadn't forgotten where it was.

He was looking about him now with rueful derision, and Juliet tried to see the house through his eyes. It was as William had always liked it, with antique furniture and furnishings, vases of fresh flowers in all the main rooms, a huge arrangement in creams and orange on a round table in this reception area. And Juliet knew that when they walked through to the family sitting-room there would be a log fire burning in the fireplace. Yes,

79

everything was still exactly as William had liked it. And she personally saw no reason to change that.

Liam, as he looked around the house he hadn't seen for ten years, didn't look quite so happy with what he saw. His expression was grim as he slowly walked about looking at things that must once have been very familiar to him—were still familiar to him—which was probably why he looked so grim!

Juliet couldn't say that she was feeling exactly happy with the way things were either, but that had nothing to do with Carlyle House.

Liam had followed through on his announcement of his intention to return with her by arranging for them both to fly back three days later. There had then been two days during which he had arrogantly ordered her to rest completely, ignoring all of her protests that she would rather return immediately now that the decision had been made. In fact, he had just ignored all her protests, period! Nothing she had said during those two days had deterred him from his decision that she rest, and although she inwardly had to admit that she was feeling slightly better she certainly hadn't enjoyed having Liam waiting on her. It made her uncomfortable to accept his attention in that way.

'Miss Juliet!' the housekeeper greeted warmly as she came through to see who the visitor was. 'How lovely. Mr Liam . . . !' Janet gasped as she saw him standing at the foot of the wide curved staircase.

'Janet,' he greeted drily. 'My God, nothing *has* changed.' He shook his head almost dazedly, striding across the distance that separated him from the housekeeper and clasping her in a bear-hug that made her gasp.

Janet Byrd, small and plump, with warm blue eyes and a head of completely white hair, had been with the Carlyle family since she had first come to the house as a maid when William had arrived with his bride. She had never married, claiming the Carlyles were the only family she wanted.

There was only Janet in the house now—and a young girl from the village who came in to help on a daily basis—but she could still tell tales of how grand it had all been forty years ago, with six household staff and a veritable army of gardeners to keep the grounds in immaculate condition. Those grounds were now kept in a similar condition by a contract gardener who came in two days a week. Almost sixty now, Janet had seen a lot of changes in the Carlyle fortunes during those forty years.

She was obviously pleased to see Liam in his old home, if a little confused. 'Why did no one tell me you were coming?' She frowned slightly reprovingly at Juliet. 'I could have got your old room ready,' she said, with a shake of her head.

Liam grimaced. 'I'm not sure whether or not I'm staying yet,' he bit out tautly as he released the elderly housekeeper. 'And, if I do, I certainly don't want my old room!'

Janet looked hurt. 'But——'

'Could we have some tea, Janet?' Juliet took over calmly, knowing by that stubborn set to Liam's mouth that he wasn't about to be pressurised into doing anything he didn't want to do—not even by the woman he must have known since his birth thirty-eight years ago. 'It's been a tiring day,' she exaggerated—the journey had been achieved so smoothly that it was difficult to realise that they were actually back in England. But Liam looked as if he had taken enough for one day; returning to Carlyle Manor was obviously a strain for him.

'I'll bring it through in just a couple of minutes.' Janet was obviously glad of something useful to do. 'It is lovely to see you back, Mr Liam,' she paused at the door to tell him.

Liam shook his head once the housekeeper had gone through to the kitchen. 'I had forgotten all about Janet,' he said, frowning.

Juliet doubted that he had actually forgotten; he had just chosen to put all memory of his family, and everything to do with them, firmly from his mind during the last ten years. Whatever the family rift had been about, and she doubted if she would ever know, it had certainly been something major.

'Thank you.'

She looked across at Liam enquiringly, not understanding the quiet comment.

'The request for tea,' he explained ruefully. 'Janet might have been hurt by my next comment,' he accepted self-deprecatingly. 'You're quite an astute little thing, aren't you?' he remarked as he strode through to the sitting-room.

'Will you stop being patronising about my size?' Juliet snapped as she almost had to run to keep up with his long strides. She had heard it all during the last few days, from 'midget' right through to 'pint-size', and quite frankly she was getting tired of it.

He turned to her with a genuinely surprised expression on his face. 'I didn't mean to be patronising.' He frowned. 'It's just—well, you can't deny you're a bit on the small side, can you?' He grimaced lamely. 'You are a bit tetchy after our journey, aren't you?' His frown returned as he looked down at her. 'Maybe we should have left it a couple more days before coming back.'

A couple more days of this man telling her what to do all the time and she would have thrown one of his trays of food at him! 'I'm perfectly all right, thank you,' she told him sharply. 'I would just appreciate your treating me like a grown woman for a change!'

'I thought I did,' he said quietly.

Juliet looked across at him as she stood near the fire; there had been something altogether too intimate in his tone of voice. And since that first morning, as she had lain in bed in her underwear, there had been no further indication that he had even realised that she was a woman—certainly no apparent return of the intensity of feeling that had been between them so fleetingly.

She swallowed hard. 'Your business partner, then,' she corrected herself awkwardly, aware that, even if there had been no further physical awareness between them during the rest of their stay in Majorca, it was certainly there now. And it was the last thing she wanted with this particular man—with any man!

'For the moment.' He nodded abruptly. 'We'll know just how viable that is once I've looked over Carlyle Properties,' he explained at her questioning look.

Juliet could only begin to guess what he meant by looking over Carlyle Properties, and, if he found it wasn't viable, exactly what he would do about it!

'You——' She broke off abruptly as Janet entered with the tea-tray, appetising-looking sandwiches also there with the tea things. 'Thank you, Janet.' She smiled her dismissal of the older woman.

'I'll get a room ready for you just in case, Mr Liam,' the housekeeper told him before she left.

Liam gave a wry smile. 'She always was a tenacious woman. My father probably should have married her years ago,' he added with a frown.

Juliet looked up from pouring the tea, the pot held poised in her hand. 'I beg your pardon?'

He steadily returned her gaze. 'Janet loved my father for years, surely you knew that?' he said derisively.

She most certainly had not, had never picked up even so much of a hint that the other woman had felt that way towards William. Although she had always thought it strange that a lovely woman like Janet, obviously a once very beautiful woman, should never have married.

'Obviously not,' Liam drawled at Juliet's stunned silence. 'Well, they do say there's none so blind...' he dismissed drily. 'Probably you just didn't want to see it. After all, it might have interfered with your own relationship with my father if you had.'

Juliet felt the colour in her cheeks. 'I have told you, repeatedly,' she said emphatically, 'that my relationship with your father was completely platonic!'

'I know.' Liam nodded mockingly. 'And I have tried, repeatedly,' he added just as emphatically, 'to believe that you really lived here, for several years, it seems, as his assistant and platonic companion.'

And he obviously still didn't believe it for one minute! Well, she wasn't about to keep saying it; after all, there was another saying, 'The lady doth protest too much, me thinks'; the more she kept denying it, the more likely Liam Carlyle was to believe it was true!

'I always assumed my father didn't return Janet's feelings because he didn't want any woman permanently in his life after my mother died,' Liam frowned. 'But as you've been here for some time that apparently wasn't the case.'

Juliet had to bite her lip to stop herself once again answering defensively. No matter what she said, Liam wasn't going to be convinced that she hadn't been involved with his father. And really, at the end of the day, she didn't care what he thought, as long as he helped her salvage Carlyle Properties.

'Poor Janet,' he added goadingly, taking his cup of tea out of Juliet's slightly shaking hand.

The housekeeper had been extremely distraught at William's death. In fact, she had been with him when he died, had taken his cup of tea up to his bedroom in the morning only to find that he had had a heart attack some time during the night. There hadn't been time to call a doctor or anything else, as William had died almost immediately. It had almost been as if he had been waiting not to be alone when he went. But Juliet had never had any idea that Janet had actually loved her employer. How awful for the other woman. And how sad that she had apparently had years of unrequited love.

But Janet knew, no matter what Liam himself might have assumed to the contrary, that there had never been anything but friendship between Juliet and William, that the elderly man had been more like a father to her than anything else. And so Juliet had no reason to defend herself before Liam. She had no reason to, but it was still very difficult *not* to.

Liam gave an impatient glance at his watch. 'Well, as it's too late to go into the office today, we'll have to leave that until the morning, so I think I'll go and shower and change before having a look around this place.' His expression was grim once again. 'Although I stand by my first statement: nothing seems to have changed!'

Except that, since he had left ten years ago, his father and brother had both died, Juliet could have pointed out. But didn't. This was all difficult enough as it was, without further antagonism between them.

'I'll get Janet to show you to your room,' she said politely as she rang for the housekeeper.

Liam watched her consideringly. 'You're pretty good at this, aren't you?' he murmured tauntingly.

She steeled herself for the insult she knew was about to come. 'Good at what?'

He shrugged. 'Being mistress of the house. Must be years of training,' he added with cold dismissal, before putting down his empty cup and striding out into the hallway to meet the housekeeper. Juliet heard the murmur of their voices seconds later.

There had been an unmistakable double edge to Liam's last statement, and, although she had been half expecting it, it was still hurtful; her hands shook as she put down her own cup of tea untouched. By 'mistress of the house' Liam meant something completely different from the usual context, and he had meant to be deliberately insulting.

He was a strange man, one minute insisting that she rest while at his villa, the next, in this house, treating her with the contempt which he thought his father's mistress deserved. But he was right about her insensitivity to Janet's feelings for William; William and Janet had always got on extremely well, more like friends than employer and employee, but it had never occurred to Juliet that there might be more to it than that on Janet's side. No wonder the other woman had been so upset at his death. Juliet felt a certain amount of guilt now where the housekeeper was concerned because of her own lack of understanding.

As no doubt Liam meant her to—although the guilt he believed she should feel was concerning her own supposed affair with his father!

Juliet busied herself in the study before dinner, dealing with any immediate business matters, only going upstairs to shower and change fifteen minutes before she knew the meal was to be served. She hadn't seen Liam since he'd left the sitting-room so abruptly after tea, and could only suppose he had business of his own he was dealing with.

She felt as if her heart had jumped into her mouth as she walked down the hallway to her bedroom only to see the door further down from her own standing slightly ajar; someone was in Simon's bedroom! Surely Janet wouldn't have chosen that room to give Liam? No, she simply couldn't believe that Janet could have been so insensitive.

But Liam could!

Juliet hurried down the hallway to stand in front of a doorway that hadn't been opened for seven years, as far as she was aware. And she still couldn't go into the room herself. She stood on the threshold looking in, watching him as he moved lightly around, looking at a room that had stayed exactly as Simon had left it.

He turned and saw her standing there; he was already dressed in a black evening suit and snowy white shirt. 'I thought I would dress for dinner,' he drawled drily as he saw her staring at him.

Juliet didn't care what he wore for dinner; she just wanted him out of this room! 'This is Simon's room,' she said stiffly.

Liam's mouth twisted. 'I'm well aware of whose room this was, Juliet,' he bit out tautly. 'My little brother obviously chose the furnishings himself!' He looked derisively about him at the glass and chrome furniture which was completely at odds with the quiet elegance of the rest of the house.

And he was right—Simon had picked all the furniture in here himself, had taken great delight in modernising his own personal domain.

'But I don't suppose you would know that, would you?' he said as he crossed the room to join her. 'He's been dead for over seven years now...' he reflected.

She knew exactly how long Simon had been dead, could have told Liam not only to the day but to the hour and minute as well.

'I do know that,' she said abruptly. 'What are you doing in here?' She didn't feel as if she could move away from the door now that it had finally been opened once again, even though she could sense that Liam wanted to leave the room.

He shrugged. 'Trying to see, from the things he left behind, whether my little brother had changed at all.'

Juliet could have told him that she was also one of 'the things' that Simon had left behind, and could have asked what looking at her told him about his brother. But the shock of seeing this room again was more than enough for one evening; she wasn't up to coping with Liam's verbal fencing concerning her past relationship with Simon as well.

Liam gave a grimace at the chrome and glass furnishings. 'He obviously hadn't!' he said disgustedly.

She couldn't say whether Simon had changed or not after Liam had left; she could only remember the Simon that she had known. 'You didn't come home for his funeral either,' she said flatly, finally managing to follow Liam from the room, closing the door firmly behind her, trembling slightly as that feeling of someone walking over her grave shivered down her spine.

He shook his head grimly. 'He was already dead and buried by the time I read about it in the newspapers.'

'And your rift with your father was so strong that you didn't feel perhaps you could do him some good by returning?' Juliet frowned.

His eyes hardened coldly. 'Nothing had changed,' he rasped harshly. 'I still wouldn't have been the son he wanted!'

'But——'

'Juliet, don't interfere in things you can't, and never will, understand,' he bit out icily.

She couldn't understand because she didn't know, but it now seemed apparent that Simon had somehow been involved in the rift between father and older son. 'I just think it's a pity that you and William couldn't have made your peace before he died.' She shrugged heavily.

Liam glanced impatiently at his watch. 'You now have five minutes to change for dinner, Juliet,' he said, lightly changing the subject. 'On past experience, I wouldn't advise you to be late for one of Janet's dinners!'

He was perfectly right about Janet's strict adherence to the times for meals, and her displeasure if her food was ruined. But Juliet didn't feel that she could eat anything even if she did manage to change in time; seeing Simon's bedroom again so suddenly like that had robbed her of all appetite.

'And don't say you don't feel like eating.' Liam correctly read her next comment, although not the reason for it. 'We've already been through that argument. Numerous times. And the doctor said I was to make sure you ate three healthy meals a day,' he added warningly.

Juliet couldn't help her gasp of laughter. 'He said I was to make sure I ate three healthy meals a day, not you!' she protested.

Liam turned her firmly in the direction of her bedroom. 'Then make sure you do. Go and change. Quickly!' he instructed firmly as she would have protested once again.

Juliet found herself in her bedroom, washing quickly, brushing her hair loosely about her shoulders, applying a light make-up, before she actually knew what she was doing. Liam was too damned fond of issuing orders—and to her chagrin she was obeying them!

She didn't want to go down to dinner; she needed time to think about finding him in Simon's bedroom like that—a bedroom that, now she thought about it, was virtually dust-free for a room that supposedly hadn't been entered for seven years... She——

'Hurry up and put your dress on, Juliet,' an all too familiar voice said from the doorway. 'We have one minute left before we're both in trouble,' Liam added warningly.

Juliet had turned sharply at the sound of his voice, staring at him wordlessly across the room. She was once again standing before him wearing only her underwear—a black bra and black lace panties this time, to go underneath the black knee-length dress she hadn't yet had time to put on.

Liam stood across the room looking at her, his sleepy blue gaze moving slowly across the golden length of her body, lingering on the deep swell of her breasts before moving down the deep curve of her waist to her hips. 'But maybe the trouble will be worth it,' he murmured as he slowly crossed the room towards her.

Juliet watched him in mute fascination, unable to move, to protest as he took her in his arms, the gasp barely out of her lips before they were claimed by his.

His mouth made a gentle exploration of hers, his arms about her bare waist, one hand moving up the length of her spine to become entwined in the

long cascade of her hair, his hand cradling her nape
as he sipped and tasted her lips.

The kiss had been so sudden, so unexpected, that
Juliet didn't have time for resistance. Her hands
tangled in the shirt at his waist, clinging to him as
he moulded the length of her body to his, his thighs
hard and powerful against her, the tip of his tongue
moistly caressing the sensitivity of her lower lip
before plunging into the warmth beyond.

Juliet felt invaded, as if the two of them were
inexplicably joined, her will completely taken from
her. If he had been roughly demanding she would
have been able to break the spell, but, as it was,
his lips and hands were sensually caressing, evoking
a response in her that she was unable to deny.

His other hand moved up the curve of her waist
to the gentle swell of her breast, cupping its
softness, the thumb-tip moving rhythmically against
the already hardened nipple. A heated warmth
flooded her thighs at the intimate caress; her whole
body felt aflame.

'You're so beautiful!' Liam groaned as his lips
left hers to travel the length of her neck and throat,
his head bending even lower as, through the flimsy
material, he took her other pert nipple into the
warm cavern of his mouth, his tongue flicking
erotically against the hardened nub.

Juliet gasped at the intimacy, her neck arched as
she pressed even closer against those pleasure-
giving lips, and almost fainted with pleasure as
Liam's hand moved to cup the warmth of her
inner thighs, his palm moving rhythmically against
her sensitivity.

This dual pleasure was almost too much to bear, her breathing ragged and shallow as she clung to his shoulders now—wide, powerful shoulders that evoked an eroticism of their own.

Liam raised his head to kiss the length of her throat once again, his lips warm and searching, his tongue flicking against a spot just below her earlobe as Juliet quivered in response. 'So deceptively innocent,' he murmured as he raised his head to look down at her with sleepy blue eyes.

Deceptively...? What...?

'Miss Juliet!' The call of her name was accompanied by a loud knock on the door. 'It's time for dinner,' Janet continued lightly. 'And I can't find Mr Liam anywhere,' she added worriedly.

The sound of Janet's voice outside her room had done the one thing Juliet seemed unable to do herself, and that was to break the sensual spell which Liam had woven about her. She pulled sharply away from him, staring up at him with stricken eyes. What had she been *doing*?

'Miss Juliet?' Janet said again, concernedly this time. 'Are you all right?'

She didn't think so; she felt devastated by the intimacy she had just shared with Liam, of all people. She avoided his gaze as she moved to grab up her towelling robe from the bedroom chair, and had just tied the belt securely about her waist when Janet, having received no answer, came worriedly into the room.

The housekeeper's eyes widened as they took in Liam's presence in Juliet's bedroom. 'You didn't answer the door, so I wasn't sure...' She trailed off awkwardly. 'Dinner is ready,' she added lamely, looking very uncomfortable.

Liam nodded curtly. 'We'll be down in a minute,' he dismissed tersely.

'I... Very well,' Janet accepted abruptly, turning away. 'I—I'm sorry if I disturbed you,' she said uneasily, closing the door firmly behind her as she left.

Oh, God, how awful! How awful that any of it had happened at all, but that Janet should now have the wrong impression about them was just terrible. Because Janet was well aware of the fact that Juliet and Liam hadn't even met until this last week!

She glanced awkwardly at Liam, not encouraged by the coldness of his expression, the derisive twist to his lips. But what right did he have to be derisive of her? He was the one who had instigated the intimacy, not she!

And it was an intimacy that made her cringe when she thought about it. There had been no one in her life since Simon—which made it all the worse that it was his older brother she had responded to!

Liam was watching her with narrowed eyes, that coldness still in his face. 'You had better dress for dinner,' he told her flatly.

She didn't want to go down to dinner now: there was no way she could sit down at the table with him as if nothing had happened between them! No way could she ever be in his company again without remembering the intimate way he had touched and caressed her. That she had allowed him to touch and caress her!

His mouth twisted as he obviously sensed her refusal to join him. 'Janet is already suspicious enough,' he bit out scornfully. 'I don't really think we need to add fuel to that particular fire by my dining alone!'

Juliet could see his point, but she really didn't see how she could have dinner with him and act as if nothing had happened.

'This has turned into a real family affair, hasn't it?' he continued mockingly, his gaze moving scathingly over Juliet's tangled hair and kiss-swollen lips.

She frowned. 'What do you mean?' It was the first time she had spoken since he had begun kissing her, and to her chagrin her voice sounded huskily low.

He shrugged. 'You said earlier you knew my brother too?'

'Yes.' She was still frowning.

'And just how well did you know dear Simon?' he taunted. 'Or did you know him before my father?'

She swallowed hard, the heat in her cheeks answer enough.

'A family affair.' He nodded coldly. 'The father and both sons—no mean feat really, is it?' he said disgustedly. 'Except that you didn't quite add me to the list. And I have no intention of allowing you to do so in the future, either,' he continued harshly. 'You just failed the test, Juliet,' he added scornfully.

She was still reeling from the insults he had just thrown at her. He couldn't really think...? But she knew by the hard derision in his face that he did! 'What test?' she asked weakly.

Liam gave a dismissive shrug. 'Whatever plans you have to draw me into this web you seem to have woven around the other Carlyle men, I advise you to forget them; this is a business affair to me. And sleeping with men may be the way you have got as far as you have, but as far as I'm concerned——'

Juliet didn't give herself time to think, didn't need time to think, her arm arching up and her hand making sharp contact with Liam's left cheek. 'Get out,' she told him forcefully. 'Just get out of my room!' Her eyes sparkled, deeply grey.

He shrugged unconcernedly. 'I wouldn't advise you to do that again either, Juliet.' The fingers of his left hand trailed pointedly down the cheek she had just slapped. 'The next time I might retaliate in kind,' he added grimly.

She stared at him, her eyes wide, feeling herself begin to sway even as the darkness threatened to engulf her.

'Oh, no, you don't,' Liam said grimly as he gripped her beneath her arms and sat her down on the bed. 'Not again,' he added harshly, looking down at her.

Juliet was recovering as quickly as the blackness had seemed to envelop her, returning Liam's gaze a little dazedly—at least she hadn't passed out again.

His mouth twisted derisively. 'Can you do that to order too, or is it just something you're developing?' he mocked harshly.

She shook her head slightly so that she could try to think clearly. 'I don't know what you mean,' she finally said weakly.

'Don't you?' he scoffed, his eyes glacial. 'Perhaps you shouldn't join me for dinner after all, Juliet.

I have a feeling that if you did I might be tempted to strangle you before the end of the meal!' he added, with self-disgust. 'You certainly evoke those sorts of emotions in me.' He shook his head. 'I would advise you to get some sleep.'

He walked over to the door. 'We're going into the office tomorrow,' he paused to tell her grimly. 'And God knows what I'm going to find out there!' He slammed out of the room.

Juliet hadn't moved—couldn't move; she could only sit on the bed and stare across the room at the door which Liam had just slammed so forcefully behind him.

Just what did he think he was going to find out at Carlyle Properties . . . ?

CHAPTER SIX

'WHY so pensive, Juliet?' Liam asked with some amusement as they approached the Carlyle offices.

They had driven into town in separate cars, Juliet having decided that she did not want to be dependent on Liam for her transportation home. But Liam had been waiting for her in the car park once she arrived, a much faster driver than she.

'I'm not pensive.' She met his gaze steadily, determined not to sound as if she was on the defensive.

The two of them had met for breakfast earlier—the first time they had seen each other since Liam's cutting remarks the night before. It had been an extremely quiet meal, with the minimum of conversation, both of them leaving for the office at eight-thirty by tacit agreement.

And Juliet wasn't pensive. She was stressed, however, and knew that a lot depended on what Liam decided today.

He raised blond brows at her as he held the door open for her to enter the building. 'Sure?' he mocked.

No, she wasn't sure; she would have liked to smack that self-assured smile right off his face! And for a person who abhorred violence . . . !

'Very. Thank you,' she bit out tautly, nodding to the girl who sat on Reception, not in the least surprised when Linda looked at Liam with frank appreciation—he seemed to have that effect on most of the female population! Including her, she acknowledged with an inward groan. But after last night she was sure that that would never happen again!

Liam looked about him critically as they moved through the building, and Juliet tried to see it through his eyes. Carlyle Properties had the bottom floor of the office building, the ten staff comprising mainly the computer department and Accounts. The offices were plushly decorated and carpeted, but that was because William had believed that it gave a better impression to clients and prospective clients, rather than because of any excess of money in the company.

She smiled at John Morgan, her assistant since William died, as he hurried down the corridor towards her, and hoped that he was going to help her today to convince Liam that the company was still viable. 'John——'

'Thank God you're here, Juliet,' he cut in, a worried look on his youthful face; at twenty-five, he had been groomed by William to help Juliet when the older man had semi-retired. 'I tried calling you at home, but Janet said you had already left, and——'

'Calm down, John,' she cut in soothingly, very conscious of Liam standing behind her, the last thing she wanted was to be met by a crisis as soon as they walked through the door!

'But you don't understand.' John was still frowning deeply. 'A Miss Gilbraith arrived about half an hour ago, and——'

'Liam?' Juliet had turned sharply towards him at the mention of his assistant's name. What was Diana Gilbraith doing here already?

'We'll talk about this in your office, Juliet,' he returned evenly, his gaze meeting hers challengingly.

For long, almost timeless moments she met that gaze, trying to read his expression. But she was wasting her time; Liam was one of the most enigmatic men she had ever met in her life!

'It's all right, John,' she turned back to assure the younger man, forcing a strained smile. 'I know who Miss Gilbraith is.' But not what she was doing here! The last she had heard of the other woman, she was having a holiday with her family...!

'You do?' John looked relieved by the information. 'Well, I wasn't sure what to do with her, so I put her in your office...' He gave a self-conscious grimace. He was tall and dark-haired, his attractive face youthfully earnest.

'Thank you, John.' Juliet gave his arm a reassuring squeeze. 'I'll talk to you later.'

'That was extremely rude of you,' Liam remarked softly once they were alone again in the corridor.

Rude of her? This man's assistant was already in the building, in her office, and he had the nerve to accuse her of being rude? He——

'You should have introduced—John?—and me,' he continued arrogantly.

She drew in an angry breath. 'I believe you should have told me Diana Gilbraith was already here!' she returned.

He shrugged unconcernedly. 'Of course Diana is here; she's my assistant.'

'And it would have been polite of you to tell me she was already here,' Juliet told him heatedly.

He gave another dismissive shrug. 'I can't see that it's important. Would you like to take me to my father's office,' he added coldly, 'and send Diana along to me there?'

Juliet's eyes widened. 'But——'

'I believe it's my office now?' Liam raised dark blond brows.

No one had used that office since William's death two months ago, but it was the obvious choice for Liam during his time here. Juliet just hoped that that time was going to be short!

'Unless you're using it now?' Liam looked down at her challengingly.

'Of course I'm not.' Juliet drew in a deep, controlling breath. This man meant to annoy her, and he could see that he was succeeding; there was a mocking glint in the dark blue of his eyes. 'That office is empty,' she told him stiffly.

His mouth tightened. 'Not any longer!'

He really was the most objectionable...! The truth of it was that she couldn't bear the thought of anyone using that office. The room represented William to her, and she could never enter it without thinking of him. It was where she had first met him, where they had spent a lot of their time together during the last seven years; the thought of Liam now using it as his office was unacceptable to her.

'Do you have a problem with that?' He continued to look at her coldly.

Yes, she had a severe problem with it! 'Not at all,' she assured him coolly. 'It's this way.' She led the way down the corridor to the last door on the right-hand side, one hand on the door-handle as she turned briefly to look at him. 'This is my office.' She indicated the door on the opposite side of the corridor.

His mouth twisted mockingly. 'How cosy!' he drawled.

She literally had to bite her bottom lip to stop the sharp comment that instantly sprang to her lips, and turned abruptly away from him to push open the door to his father's—his!—office.

As with the house, this room was decorated and furnished in the style that William liked; the desk and accompanying chairs were antique, the walls papered a muted green, the carpet the same shade of green. The green leather desktop was bare now, but during William's day it had been littered with paperwork—paperwork that was now in Juliet's office, where Diana Gilbraith had been waiting for the last half an hour.

'I'll send Miss Gilbraith——' Juliet turned to leave the room so sharply that she walked straight into Liam as he stood behind her. She stared up at him wordlessly, their bodies almost touching.

'I don't know how you've behaved in the past, Juliet, but I don't approve of that sort of thing in the office!' he rasped harshly, clasping the tops of her arms to put her firmly out of his way as he walked further into the room. 'And when you get into your office would you ask Diana to come in here?' he added by way of dismissal, moving to sit in the high-backed chair behind the desk.

Juliet was glad to escape from the room; she couldn't bear the sight of him sitting in the chair which William used to occupy. She wished, not for the first time, that she had never gone to Majorca, had never found Edward William Carlyle at all!

Except, as she very well knew, she hadn't exactly found Liam at all; he had found her. And he had been playing games with her ever since!

She took a deep, steadying breath before opening the door to her office and standing in the doorway to look across the room to where Diana Gilbraith sat, not, as Juliet had assumed, behind her desk but on the opposite side of it.

Diana looked up with a warm, friendly smile, a file open on her knee as she sat with her elegantly curved legs neatly crossed. 'Hello again.' She stood up in one smooth movement. 'Are you feeling better now?'

Juliet wasn't quite sure what she had expected when she entered her office, but it certainly hadn't been this woman's friendliness! And as far as she could see none of the papers on her desk had been disturbed.

She stared at the other woman blankly. 'Better?' she repeated with a frown.

'Hmm,' Diana nodded, her blonde hair as neatly styled as usual, her skin still tanned from the time she had recently spent in Majorca. 'When Liam telephoned me yesterday he explained that the reason he had been delayed was that you hadn't been too well. I must say you have a bit more colour in your cheeks than the last time I saw you,' she added encouragingly.

Juliet wasn't too sure of this woman's friendliness. After all, Diana did work for Liam. Maybe she was just lulling her into a false sense of security!

'I spent several days in the sun,' she answered vaguely. 'Er—Liam is in the office across the corridor,' she added, her voice hardening at the mere mention of his name. 'He would like you to join him.'

Diana nodded lightly, her blue eyes still warm. 'I'll probably see you later, then.' She left the room with a smile.

Juliet closed the door thankfully behind the other woman before moving to sit behind her desk, letting out a sigh as she did so, relieved to be on her own again.

She should have known Liam was a businessman through and through; he hadn't succeeded in his own business without being extremely competent at what he did. And ruthless. God knew what hornets' nest she had opened up by seeking him out and having him come here. But she couldn't possibly have known he would want to come here personally to investigate the company; she had assumed that he would send an assistant, someone like Diana Gilbraith, to come and check things out. But then, she hadn't known Liam Carlyle and the type of man he was...

'It would appear that this is the office to be in!'

Juliet was startled by Liam's intrusion, looking up sharply from the file she had been working on. 'But this is my office.' She frowned her puzzlement. What was it? Didn't he like the view from William's office?

The door across the corridor from her own had remained firmly shut during the forty-five minutes since Diana Gilbraith had entered it, and after fifteen minutes of sitting at her desk waiting for some sort of reaction from Liam—she wasn't even sure what!—Juliet had decided to get on with some of the work on her desk that had accumulated since she left for Majorca nearly two weeks ago.

Whatever Liam had been doing in the last forty-five minutes, he didn't look very happy! Juliet tensed guardedly.

After closing the door with quiet purpose behind him, Liam strode forcefully into the room, looking about him curiously as he did so. Juliet's office was decorated in blue and white—white walls, dark blue carpet, her dark wood desk and chair serviceable rather than richly ornate as William's office furniture was. She preferred to work in this more clinical atmosphere, felt comforted by the starkness of the room. But somehow Liam managed to make her feel uncomfortable about it as he stood across the desk from her looking down at her with such superiority!

She sat back, determined not to be intimidated. 'I don't think this room altogether meets with your approval,' she recognised drily.

He gave a dismissive shrug of those broad shoulders beneath the pale blue shirt, having removed the jacket to his dark blue suit. 'I don't care one way or the other,' he asserted scornfully. 'My comment referred to the fact that my father's office appears to be empty of all relevant information concerning Carlyle Properties!' He looked down at her with raised brows.

She had known it wouldn't take him long to realise that—in fact, she was surprised it had taken this long! She hadn't wanted to work directly from

William's office after his death, and so the logical
thing to do had been to move all the files into her
office. It had taken her and John a day to do it,
but everything was now filed away in the cabinets
that lined one wall of her office.

Liam saw her quick glance in their direction. 'Do
we move them back, or do you want me to work
from here?' He turned back to her challengingly.

She most certainly did not want him working in
here, and he knew it, damn him! 'I've asked John
to come to my office,' she answered him calmly
enough. 'We'll move all the relevant information
into Will—your office later this morning.' There
was a slightly haunted look in her eyes at the acceptance that the office opposite this one now belonged to Liam.

He shook his head, his expression grim. 'That
isn't good enough, I'm afraid,' he bit out tersely.

He wasn't 'afraid' at all—just very determined
to have things the way he wanted them. And that
included the Carlyle files! 'I——' She broke off abruptly, looking towards the doorway as John
Morgan entered her office after the briefest of
knocks.

'Juliet, rumour has it——' John broke off just
as abruptly, looking very uncomfortable as he saw
the other man standing in the room.

Liam looked at him speculatively, his stance relaxed, fully relaxed. Which the other two people in
the room certainly weren't, Juliet freely acknowledged. John looked uncertain of himself and the
situation, and Juliet didn't even try to hide the fact
that she wasn't happy with it either!

'Rumour has it . . . ?' Liam prompted softly, his dark blue gaze fixed steadily on the younger man.

John recovered quickly, straightening slightly, although there was still a slightly uncomfortable flush to his cheeks. 'Rumour has it that you're Edward Carlyle,' he announced.

Juliet couldn't help but admire John's outward calm; he might be quaking inside—Liam certainly had that effect on people!—but on the surface the younger man now looked completely composed. William's choice of John over other applicants for the job of junior assistant seemed to have been well calculated.

Liam nodded abruptly. 'I am,' he confirmed shortly. 'But my friends call me Liam,' he continued less harshly, holding out his hand in greeting. 'Which is probably why Juliet calls me anything *but* Liam!' he added tauntingly, glancing at her, his brows raised mockingly.

John didn't look too sure about the latter remark, but he willingly shook the older man's hand. 'John Morgan,' he supplied. 'I was your father's——'

'Junior assistant.' Liam nodded tersely. 'The one thing that did seem to have been left in my father's office was a file on personnel,' he said coldly, reminding Juliet that little else had been left.

Her mouth tightened at the unspoken rebuke. 'Your father and I both had copies of that file so there was no need for the duplication in my office,' she returned defiantly.

'Hmm.' Liam nodded slowly, steadily meeting the cool grey of her gaze with one equally cold. 'I thought it must be something like that,' he dismissed scathingly. 'Nice to meet you, John,' he said more warmly to the younger man. 'I'm sure you and my father worked well together. I hope we can do the same.'

Juliet gave him a sharp look. What did he mean by that remark? Surely, if Liam agreed to keep the company running, he intended being a silent partner? Although, somehow, she doubted Liam had ever been silent about anything in his life!

'To continue our conversation,' Liam interrupted her musings hardly, the warmth gone from his voice as he spoke to her, 'later this morning isn't good enough,' he repeated firmly.

She had already guessed that from his earlier reaction. 'Look, Liam . . .' she deliberately used his name, if only to show that she did call him that too '. . . I've been out of the office for almost two weeks. I have a lot of catching up to do.' She indicated the pile of paperwork on her desk.

'There are two of us here now, Juliet,' he bit out coldly. 'And the sooner I'm familiar with the workings and dealings of the company, the better I'll be able to help you deal with the backlog.'

Grey eyes clashed with deep blue ones as the two of them visually duelled. Juliet was very aware of John in the room with them, and knew it put her at a disadvantage; without his presence she might have been better able to deal with this situation. Might. But somehow she doubted it! It was not her intention that Liam should help her deal with anything, let alone the workings of Carlyle Properties.

Finally it was her gaze that dropped, and she turned to John instead. 'Do you have time to help me with this, John?' She sounded clam, but inside she was seething.

Liam had spoken to her as if she were half-witted! Of course she knew he would have to know about the company—he couldn't make a judgement without that knowledge—but it had never been her intention that he should actually help her run it, even on a temporary basis. And he could have been more diplomatic in his approach... That was rather stupid of her, she thought; the words 'diplomatic' and 'Liam' could never be used together!

'Of course.' John was still frowning, obviously sensing the hostility between Juliet and Liam and not feeling quite sure of his own place in the midst of it.

She turned back to Liam. 'We'll see to your request as quickly as possible,' she informed him distantly. 'As soon as I've dealt with anything on my desk that needs my immediate attention,' she added stubbornly; she was not about to drop everything else in order to jump to this man's bidding.

His mouth thinned with displeasure, his deep blue eyes narrowing coldly at what he knew to be her deliberate evasion. 'Very well,' he finally nodded abruptly, and strode over to the door.

Juliet breathed a sigh of relief at his imminent departure.

'One more thing, Juliet.' Liam paused at the open doorway, his gaze unblinking as he looked across the distance of the room at her.

She knew from the determination of his expression that she had breathed that sigh of relief too soon. 'Yes?' she prompted warily.

'I realise that it will take you some time to organise the bulk of the files back across the corridor,' he acknowledged. 'But there's one account I would like you to send over immediately.'

Juliet frowned. As far as she was aware, Liam hadn't been involved with the company for at least ten years, so how could he now be asking for a specific account?

'It's ten years old, so you may have to get it from the store-room in the basement.' He shrugged. 'I take it you still store dead accounts down there?'

'Yes,' Juliet confirmed dazedly. She was totally thrown by his request; what possible interest could he have in a project that was ten years old?

He nodded tersely. 'I'd like the Walters account from December of that year,' he instructed abruptly before leaving as suddenly as he had entered a few minutes ago.

Had it been only a few minutes ago? Juliet had the feeling of having been swept along in a whirlwind for timeless minutes. She...

'Wow.' John dazedly echoed her sentiments. 'So that's the long-lost son.' He shook his head as he sat down in the chair opposite Juliet. 'Not quite what I expected,' he said speculatively.

He wasn't quite what Juliet had expected either, which was why she hadn't initially made any connection between Edward Carlyle and the Liam she had met in Majorca. She wished she still hadn't!

And there was still the puzzle of why he wanted the Walters file. Of course he had still been here himself then, and might have been involved in the project, but even so it still seemed a very strange request to her.

She was curious to see that file now herself, and fully intended looking through it thoroughly before passing it on to Liam. She had quickly learnt that Liam Carlyle didn't do anything without purpose. There had to be a reason why he wanted that specific file. And she doubted very much that he intended telling her what it was!

CHAPTER SEVEN

NOTHING. Absolutely nothing. The store-room downstairs had been checked, double-checked, and then checked again. By John Morgan. There was no Walters file.

But Liam had sounded so definite. And, as Juliet was learning, he was rarely wrong. So finally, out of desperation, she had gone down to the store-room herself. After half an hour's fruitless search she had to concede that John was right—there was no Walters file.

But if there had been a client called Walters then there had to be a file, and if, as Liam had said, the account was ten years old, then the file would be down in the store-room; any file over five years old was automatically put downstairs at the end of the financial year. It was what William had always done.

But there was no Walters file downstairs!

A search of the filing cabinets in her own office had revealed no such file either, and quite frankly Juliet was at a loss to know what to do now. The first thing Liam asked her to supply him with concerning the company and she couldn't even find it. Wonderful!

Over an hour had passed since he had made the request, and, being Liam, he surely wouldn't wait much longer for the file to materialise in his office. Should she attack, by going to him and telling him that he must have made a mistake, or should she sit in her office and wait for him to come to her? The latter choice put her at a definite disadvantage where a man like him was concerned. And there was always the possibility that he might have made a mistake. A remote one, she inwardly acknowledged heavily, but it was a possibility.

Two golden heads were bent over William's green leather-topped desk when Juliet entered the room after a brief knock, but not on opposite sides of the desk, as one might have expected; Diana and Liam were sitting close together behind it. Diana looked up and smiled as Juliet entered. Liam just scowled at the intrusion.

And that was exactly how Juliet felt—like an intruder! These two were obviously very close—and not just by locality. Juliet couldn't help wondering how Liam viewed 'that sort of thing' out of the office!

He sat back in the high-backed leather chair, looking across at Juliet with narrowed eyes. 'Yes?' He looked pointedly at her empty hands.

She moistened her lips. 'Er—there doesn't seem to be a Walters file.' Very dynamic! So much for attack; she sounded like an apprehensive schoolgirl. She straightened her shoulders determinedly. 'Are you sure you have the right name?'

Liam's mouth tightened. 'Positive.'

She had thought he might be! 'We can carry on looking, of course. There's always the possibility that it might have been mis-filed.' She gave a rueful shrug.

'How convenient!' His mouth twisted bitterly.

Juliet frowned. 'Look, it was ten years ago, Liam,' she reasoned impatiently. God, she hadn't even worked for the company then. 'You *could* have the wrong name——'

'No,' he cut in harshly, 'I couldn't. Did my father keep any of the paperwork anywhere else? At the house, perhaps?'

Her frown deepened at his persistence. After all, the account was ten years old anyway, was dead and buried. Literally so, it appeared. But things like this happened in a company as big and strong as Carlyle Properties had once been. No doubt the file would turn up some time—William had been too thorough in his records for it to be any other way—but at the moment she just couldn't find it.

'William occasionally worked from the house, yes,' she began slowly. 'But——'

'Then we'll look there,' he interrupted curtly.

What was so special about the Walters file that he was so determined to find it? Before he had walked out on the family and the business Liam had worked for the company, Juliet knew that, so perhaps it had been a pet project of his and he wanted to see how it had worked out. But, even so, surely they had much more pressing matters to deal with just now than a project that was ten years old!

'What exactly was the Walters account?' She was still frowning at him.

'A six-storeyed office building,' he bit out grimly.

Juliet looked at him expectantly, thinking there had to be more. But he said nothing else, just met her gaze with a steady challenge. But Juliet was puzzled. Carlyle Properties had put up lots of office blocks in the eight years she had been with the company, either under contract, or building them themselves for selling. What was so special about this one building?

Oh, God, she had given up trying to sort out the workings of Liam's mind; she just had to find this file as quickly as possible. Maybe it was at the house, although she couldn't for the life of her understand why it should be.

'I see,' she nodded, but, of course, didn't see at all. But it was a minor point as far as she was concerned. 'John and I are ready to move the other files back in here now,' she added.

'I'll help you,' Diana offered warmly.

There was no such offer forthcoming from Liam, Juliet noticed, tensing warily as he stood up to cross the width of the office to her side. She tensed even more as one of his hands was raised towards her.

'A cobweb,' he drawled mockingly as he removed the gossamer web from her hair, lightly brushing her temple with his fingertips as he did so.

Juliet felt colour warm her cheeks. What had she thought he was going to do, especially with Diana Gilbraith as their audience?

'Thank you,' she said huskily, pushing her hair back from her face, wondering if there were any other signs of her search of the basement.

His mouth twisted derisively as he looked down at her with amused eyes. 'You're welcome,' he murmured softly.

Juliet turned away abruptly, looking across at the other woman, inwardly wondering what Diana was making of all this. Probably she was too discreet

where her employer was concerned to think anything of his behaviour!

'See to those letters for me, Diana.' Liam spoke
to his assistant in a businesslike tone. 'I'll see you
later. Both of you,' he added drily.

Juliet frowned as he strode from the office. It
was too early for lunch; surely he hadn't gone off
for the rest of the day? Left alone with Diana, she
didn't like to ask the other woman, and Diana,
being the sort of discreet personal assistant Liam
was likely to have chosen, didn't volunteer any information concerning her employer's movements
either.

By lunchtime they had moved the bulk of the
files back into William's office. And Liam still
hadn't returned. Maybe he wasn't going to, Juliet
thought as she took a working lunch in her own
office. Actually, it was an apple and half a cheese
sandwich which she had bought from the cafeteria
in the building. Unlike Liam, she didn't have time
to go out for leisurely lunches.

As usual, her office door stood open, and she
looked up as Diana came to stand there. She had
come to like the other woman more and more as
the morning had progressed, had found her to be
cheerful and hard-working, with infinite patience
for getting things right. No doubt she would need
that, working for Liam!

Diana looked disappointed as she saw the re-
mains of the cheese sandwich on Juliet's desk. 'I
thought perhaps you might like to come to lunch
with me,' she said ruefully. 'But I can see you've
already eaten.' She shrugged. 'You could always sit
and have dessert with me?' she added hopefully.

Juliet was about to refuse, and then changed her mind. She hadn't taken a break all morning, and even if she only had a coffee with the other woman it was better than nothing. If Diana and Liam were going to be around for any length of time, it would be helpful if she could get on with at least one of them! Besides, it couldn't be much fun for Diana either, just being thrown in at the deep end here. No doubt the other woman was more than capable of taking care of herself, but it would still be rather rude of Juliet to refuse her invitation.

'Dessert sounds good.' She returned the other woman's smile, standing up to collect her jacket from behind the door. 'There's a nice French restaurant around the corner that used to serve lovely pastries.' She and William had occasionally gone there to reward themselves if they had been working particularly hard.

The restaurant was very busy, as usual, but they managed to find a table for two, and as they sat down Juliet started to wonder what they were actually going to talk about. Liam was obviously off limits, and Juliet had never been particularly forthcoming about her own background, so that really only left Diana's family.

'Were your family pleased to see you home last week?' she asked the other woman conversationally; most women, she assumed, would be quite happy to talk about their children, although never having had any herself, she didn't really know.

'Actually they're my stepchildren—a boy and a girl from Tom's first marriage—so we usually only have them at weekends,' Diana supplied easily. 'I left it rather late in life to get married—too much of a career woman,' she added with a grimace.

'You and Tom don't want any of your own?' Juliet asked curiously.

'Well, actually——' Diana broke off as the waiter came to take their order. 'Just coffee and pastries, isn't it, Juliet?' she prompted, nodding confirmation to the waiter once Juliet had given her tacit approval.

'Wouldn't you like more than that?' Juliet frowned once they were alone again. 'Don't not have anything just because I've already eaten.'

Diana gave a lightly dismissive laugh. 'I'm trying not to put on too much weight. You see——'

'Not another woman obsessed with her weight,' an all too familiar voice cut in derisively. 'John told me this was where I could find you both,' Liam explained his presence beside their table as Juliet gave him a startled look.

She couldn't quite believe he was here; she was starting to feel haunted by this man. But she always informed John where she was going when she left the office, so she supposed this was her own fault.

'Going to join us?' Diana invited warmly, seemingly unaware of any tension between Juliet and Liam.

'If Juliet doesn't mind.' He looked down at her with those piercing blue eyes.

What did he expect her to reply to that? He obviously knew what reply she would like to make; he also knew that she wouldn't be that rude in front of a third person. 'Of course not,' she answered graciously, even though it was the last thing she really wanted. She had a feeling she and Diana

Gilbraith were going to get along just fine, and she felt more than a little resentful of Liam's interruption of their conversation.

Being at a small table for two, which was now having a third place laid at it so that Liam could also eat, the three of them were sitting rather close together, and Juliet moved away sharply when her knee inadvertently made contact with Liam's under the table as he sat down.

He gave her an amused look at her reaction. 'Sorry,' he murmured drily, moving his chair back slightly so that his legs weren't so far under the table.

What was it about this man that put her so much on edge? He had had that effect on her even before she had known who he was, but the feeling had only increased since she had found out his identity. And it didn't help that she seemed to respond to him physically in a way that she found totally disturbing!

'I'll have whatever the ladies are having,' Liam told the waiter when he came for his order.

Diana looked at him with amused blue eyes once they were all alone again. 'You may change your mind once you see what we've ordered!' she told him teasingly.

He gave her an easy smile. 'Probably,' he accepted wryly. 'So you thought the two of you had earned a break?' he added mockingly. 'Work all done, is it?'

Juliet opened her mouth to give him a cutting reply—at least some of them had been working this morning!—but Diana got in before her.

'Slave-driver!' she told him good-naturedly.

'Possibly,' he conceded dismissively. 'I've been back to the house, Juliet, the file isn't in my father's desk. And the filing cabinet there is locked.'

Juliet just stared at him. He had been back to the house this morning? She didn't understand. What was so special about this particular file? Pet project of his or not, it seemed rather extreme!

'I have the key,' she told him dazedly.

He nodded as if he had already guessed that. 'Can I have it, please?' He held out his hand pointedly.

She frowned. The filing cabinet in William's office held all his private papers; he hadn't believed in safes, because he'd thought that they just encouraged people to think that there was something worth stealing. So he had always put important papers in the filing cabinet in his study in the house.

Of course, William might have left the house to her, but things like his personal papers must surely belong to Liam. Nevertheless, she still felt reluctant to give Liam the key to the cabinet.

'It's back in my office,' she answered evasively, at the same time feeling as if Liam might be able to see into her handbag, see the key in a zipped pocket there.

He met her gaze challengingly, as if he had guessed exactly that. But other than calling her an actual liar... 'I'll have it later, then,' he finally answered, sitting back as the waiter arrived with their coffee and pastries. 'I see what you mean,' he said ruefully, looking at the sweet, sickly food.

'I did warn you,' Diana laughed at his expression.

There was such an easy camaraderie between these two, and yet Juliet was still convinced that her second impression of them was the correct one—there was nothing romantic between them. Maybe there had been once, a long time ago, and that accounted for their easy familiarity with each other, but it was certainly over now. Besides, she and William had been the best of friends and there had never been anything between them either—no matter what Liam might think to the contrary!

He turned probing blue eyes on her just as she was about to eat a forkful of sticky pastry. 'Has the first day been as bad as you thought it would be?' he asked drily.

The pastry never got as far as her mouth as she stared at him; what did he mean, 'the first day'? Just how long did he and Diana intend to be at Carlyle Properties?

'That's hardly a fair question to ask her in front of me, Liam,' Diana reproved lightly, having no qualms about eating her own pastry, and obviously relishing its sweetness.

He raised dark blond brows. 'I don't ever remember telling Juliet I was going to be fair,' he drawled mockingly.

He hadn't told her that he was going to be anything—that was the trouble! She just didn't know what was going on when this man was about.

'To answer your question,' she said quietly, 'if I knew what you wanted from Carlyle Properties, perhaps I could be more helpful.'

His eyes took on a glacial sheen. 'The truth,' he bit out harshly. 'That's what I want from Carlyle Properties!'

She frowned across at him. 'Carlyle Properties has nothing to hide,' she told him slowly, giving up on the pastry, her appetite once again deserting her. 'Everything is up to date. You're perfectly free to go to any of our work sites, view any of the paperwork——' She broke off as she realised that there was one file he couldn't view, for the simple reason that she couldn't find it. And that appeared to be the only one he was interested in!

'Exactly.' Liam nodded abruptly at her hesitation.

Her eyes glowed, deep grey. 'What is so special about this one file, Liam?' she snapped.

'I believe that is my business,' he returned icily. 'Literally. You weren't even involved in the company then!'

Juliet was very aware of Diana as their audience, a Diana who seemed slightly nonplussed by Liam's aggressive attitude towards her.

She put down her fork, giving up any pretence of eating; she was only here at all because she had thought she was keeping Diana company. Now that Liam was here that was no longer necessary. And she certainly didn't want to spend any more time in his company!

'Then perhaps I had better not waste any more time, and should go back to the office to carry on looking for the damned file!' Her own anger was barely contained.

'Perhaps you had better,' he agreed forcefully, his gaze never wavering from her angrily flushed face.

'Liam——'

'Stay out of this, Diana,' he advised her hardly, not even glancing at her. 'You just don't understand.'

'You're right, I don't,' she acknowledged in a puzzled voice. 'I've never seen——'

'This is between Juliet and me,' he cut in harshly. 'Isn't it?' he prompted her coldly.

It certainly was, but she wasn't quite sure what 'it' was! When they weren't angry with each other they appeared to be in each other's arms—and neither of those situations was what she particularly wanted. How could they possibly sort out the business side of things when they were always so angry with each other? And as for being in Liam's arms...! That just clouded the issue.

Juliet bent to pick up her bag—the bag containing the key Liam had asked for... 'I'll see you both back at the office,' she said stiltedly, standing up.

Diana gave her a sympathetic grimace. 'Thanks for joining me for lunch.'

Juliet gave her first genuine smile since Liam had joined them. 'I enjoyed it.' Until they had been interrupted! 'Perhaps we can do it again some time before you leave?'

'Don't worry.' Liam was the one to answer with soft menace. 'You girls will have plenty of time to go out to lunch together again; I have a feeling we're going to be at Carlyle Properties for some time!'

Juliet didn't answer him, just walked away, her back ramrod-straight as she crossed the restaurant to the door. Just how long was 'some time' going to be? However long it was, it was going to be too long as far as she was concerned! And she didn't just have Liam all day at the office; he was actually at the house too. Wonderful!

Except he wasn't at the house that evening. Juliet returned from the office on her own at six o'clock, Liam and Diana having left some time during the afternoon and not come back. And Liam didn't return for dinner either, leaving Juliet to face Janet alone.

It was the first time she had seen the housekeeper on her own since the older woman had come into her bedroom the evening before and found Liam there too. Although Juliet knew her well enough to know that Janet wouldn't mention that fact if she didn't—and she had no intention of doing so—she nevertheless felt slightly embarrassed at facing her again.

'Mr Liam rang to say that he won't be back until much later this evening,' Janet told her as she served the soup.

Well, he could have told her that too—then she wouldn't have spent the whole afternoon dreading seeing him again!

'He always was a thoughtful young man,' Janet lingered to remember fondly. 'And he was a lovely little boy.'

Of course, Janet had been here long enough to remember that. Strangely, Juliet couldn't think of Liam as ever having been a 'lovely little boy'!

Janet's expression clouded slightly. 'It was a pity he and his father argued so much when he was older. Of course Simon——' She broke off awkwardly. 'Well, a lot of young men argue with their fathers; it's all part of the male ego,' she amended dismissively.

Juliet looked at the older woman curiously. 'Is it?' she prompted softly. She had to admit she was curious about the relationship which the three men had once had. She had known them all as individuals, but somehow couldn't quite imagine them as a family. Of course, Liam had been several years older than Simon, so the two of them had probably had little in common, but they had still been brothers, and it was a relationship that she found hard to imagine.

'Oh, yes.' Janet nodded knowledgeably. 'My own brothers were horrors during their teenage years, arguing with anyone and everyone.'

'Did Liam and Simon argue?' she asked.

'Like cat and dog.' Janet sighed heavily. 'William—Mr William was always having to get in between the two of them. I think he thought they might kill each other one day if he didn't.' She shook her head at the memory.

Juliet tried to imagine Liam and Simon, five years apart in age, as two hotheaded young men. Simon had always been a bit wild, which was why William had been so pleased when he seemed to settle down slightly in his relationship with Juliet, but somehow she could never imagine Liam as a wild young man; he looked as if he had always had a wise head on young shoulders. Or maybe it was just the way he always looked so damned superior!

And Juliet hadn't missed the way that the housekeeper had slipped up and called her former employer William. Perhaps Liam was right after all about Janet's feelings towards William, although she doubted whether Janet would appreciate her prying into those feelings now.

'Instead of which it was William and Liam who argued, causing Liam to leave,' Juliet said thoughtfully.

'Only because—— Well, it's water under the bridge now,' Janet said briskly, straightening. 'Eat your soup before it gets cold,' she instructed firmly before leaving the room.

Juliet was used to the other woman's proprietorial manner by now, knew that it was really Janet that ran the household, and that she had done so for years. And, realising now how Janet had felt towards William, Juliet could only sympathise with the other woman's situation.

But she would have liked Janet to talk further about what had happened ten years ago, would have liked to know what had really happened. She knew William had regretted it, whatever it was, but even so he had never tried to heal that breach with his older son. Until his death. And now it was all too late.

Janet made it more than obvious by her manner, when she served the main course, that she had no intention of continuing the conversation, and so Juliet ate the rest of her meal in contemplative silence.

She intended going to William's study once she had eaten, to see if she could find this file that Liam seemed to want so badly. She had been putting off the moment when she would have to look through William's desk; his study was another room she found it painful to enter, and she hadn't been near his desk in the house since he had died. But if she didn't do it then Liam would, and somehow she found that thought even more unpalatable.

It felt as bad as she had thought it would. All of William's personal papers were in his desk, and to look through them was like reading someone's private diary. Consequently, Juliet kept her search to a minimum; after all, the file had to be of a certain size, and it certainly wasn't locked away in the small box in the bottom drawer of the desk where she knew William had kept really personal things.

However, there was a large brown envelope beneath the box, of a very similar shape to the drawer itself, so that at first Juliet thought it was a drawer liner, but as none of the other drawers had a liner she realised it couldn't be that.

The name Walters fairly leapt off the top of the first piece of paper that Juliet drew out of the envelope, and she felt her heart sink. It was the Walters file. And what was this single file doing hidden away in William's private desk?

Even after reading all the documents inside, Juliet was no closer to answering that question!

It all looked perfectly in order to her—a project that William had supervised himself from start to finish, the building finished on time, all bills paid, all contracts honoured. So why was this file so important to Liam?

'Burning the midnight oil?'

She looked up with a guilty start at the sound of his voice. The only light in the room came from the desk-lamp that stood on one side of William's desk. Liam looked dark and ominous as he stood in the open doorway.

He was still wearing the suit and shirt he had worn all day, although the formal tie was missing now and the top button of his shirt undone. 'Isn't it a little late still to be working?' He moved with cat-like grace further into the room, the single light throwing his face into dark shadow, giving him a menacing appearance.

Juliet glanced briefly at the clock on the wall. Midnight. She had had no idea it was that late! She must have been poring over this file for over two hours. And she was still none the wiser!

She sat back tiredly, her shoulders aching from where she had been leaning over for so long. 'Did you have a good evening?' she said politely—distantly, she hoped. It had been a long evening, and she had no wish to prolong this conversation more than was necessary. If she had heard him enter the house it probably wouldn't have been taking place at all—she would have made sure that he hadn't found her here. But he moved with all the quiet and grace of a jungle cat, so that she never seemed to hear his approach.

'Not particularly,' he rasped, sitting on the edge of the desk to look down at her.

What did that mean? She supposed it all depended on whom he had spent the evening with; if it had been a woman he was home very early, probably hadn't expected to be back at all. She couldn't help but feel curious about the fact that there must be a woman in his life somewhere. He was too sexually attractive for it to be any other way.

'I'm sorry.' She frowned, not knowing what else to say.

'Are you?' he derided sceptically. 'Just how much did Diana tell you at lunchtime before I arrived and interrupted your cosy little chat?'

Diana? What did Diana have to do with the fact that his evening hadn't been very successful? She knew that she had had her suspicions concerning the two of them, but Diana had talked so lovingly about her family today that she had become convinced that she had to be wrong about that. Surely Liam wasn't now saying that she hadn't been wrong at all?

'We had only just arrived and ordered, ourselves,' Juliet told him stiffly.

He nodded abruptly. 'I have no objection to the two of you having lunch together, but I do not want my private affairs discussed,' he said coldly.

Juliet stared up at him. 'We didn't discuss your private affairs!' she gasped indignantly.

He stood up. 'I'm just reiterating that I don't want you to do so. Diana has always been extremely discreet, but she could be put in an awkward position where you're concerned, given the circumstances.'

'What circumstances?' Juliet could feel the anger building up inside her.

'You are, at the moment, my business partner,' he shrugged dismissively.

Juliet didn't miss that 'at the moment'. Did that mean he had already come to some sort of decision concerning Carlyle Properties?

But she was being side-tracked; she had no doubt that, whatever decision Liam had come to about the company, he would only tell her it in his own time. For now she had another issue to deal with.

'I'm sure—in the circumstances!—both Diana and I can be relied on not to talk about your private life.' She bristled. 'Diana obviously knows better, and I, quite frankly, am not particularly interested in it!' Her eyes glittered with anger as she looked up at him.

'Aren't you?' he challenged softly. 'That wasn't the impression you gave last night!'

She could feel the colour receding from her cheeks. Last night had been—well, she didn't quite know what had happened between them last night. It was an incident which she would rather forget had ever happened at all!

Liam's mouth turned back scornfully. 'You don't even know if I'm married or not!' he said sneeringly.

Hadn't he said he wasn't, back when they'd first met? Had he been lying?

She knew little about his private life since he had left here ten years ago, she admitted that, but surely she would have known if he was married? There had been no woman with him, other than Diana, in Majorca, and so she had assumed . . .

But she shouldn't have assumed anything; not all wives travelled on business with their husbands. In fact, if there were children involved in the marriage too, that would be extremely difficult to do. Children. Oh, God, she just hadn't thought . . .

'Relax, Juliet,' Liam taunted as he watched the deepening expression of horror on her face. 'I'm not married. At least,' he added softly, 'I'm not any more.'

He had been married! Were there children? Where was his wife now? Did he . . . ?

'What is it, Juliet? Do you draw the line at married men?' he taunted when he saw her stricken expression. 'No future there, hmm?' he added scornfully. 'Very few men actually leave their wives for the mistress. It's a fact of life that mistresses have a pretty raw deal.' He shrugged unconcernedly.

She couldn't find any reply; she was still reeling from the possibility that he might have been a married man with children. It had never even occurred to her . . . !

'But not "companions", hmm?' he continued remorselessly. 'They seem to fare a lot better!' He looked about the room appreciatively. 'Big houses, half-shares in the business.' His glacial gaze returned to the paleness of her face. 'Not bad for a girl from the——'

'That is enough!' Juliet stood up forcefully, a nerve pulsing in her throat as she glared at him.

His mouth was a thin, angry line. 'Believe me, I haven't even started!' he grated evenly. 'Strange, I never thought of my father as a gullible man,' he mused harshly. 'But they say there's no fool like an old fool. In my father's case, that appears to have been the case!' He shook his head disgustedly. 'But I'm neither old nor a fool, so it isn't going to work on me, Juliet.'

'I don't want anything to "work on" you,' she protested heatedly. 'William left me those things because he wanted to, not because of any supposed relationship between us. The only relationship between us was like that of father and daughter.' And it would have been a factual relationship if her marriage to Simon had had the chance to take place.

'Really?' Liam returned drily. His insulting tone was unmistakable.

'You——'

'What is this?' Liam ignored her outburst to reach past her to the desk behind.

Juliet turned to see what had so suddenly caught his interest. Colour flooded her cheeks as he looked at her with coldly accusing eyes after picking up the Walters file. She had been going to give him the file, for goodness' sake, she just hadn't had the opportunity to do so yet; he had been attackingly offensive more or less from the moment he had entered the study!

'I found the file in William's desk——'

'And decided to have a look through it yourself before giving it to me,' he said harshly. 'Find anything interesting?' he challenged.

Nothing at all. It was a file like any other file in the Carlyle Properties archives. The only thing that made it any different from the others was that it had been kept in the bottom drawer of William's desk here.

Liam closed the file with a firm snap. 'I'll take this now,' he rasped coldly. 'And I'll see you at breakfast in the morning.'

Juliet was left standing alone in the shadows of the study, feeling as if she had just been tossed around by a whirlwind!

CHAPTER EIGHT

'LIAM won't be in today,' Diana told her brightly as she looked into Juliet's office the next morning.

Juliet had spent most of the night lying awake; she had found it impossible to sleep after that conversation with Liam in the study. And, wanting to avoid him this morning, she had had coffee in her bedroom, missing breakfast altogether, only to discover from Janet, when she had gone down, that Liam had left the house very early that morning. And now it seemed that he was to be away all day. Her relief was mixed up with a certain amount of curiosity as to where he had gone.

'Business?' she asked casually, looking up from the work on her desk.

'With Liam, who knows?' Diana gave a dismissive shrug. 'I'll just carry on going through the papers you gave us yesterday,' was her parting comment as she closed Juliet's office door behind her.

Liam was right; Diana was very discreet! Had he found something in that file last night that she just hadn't seen when she had looked through it? What was he looking for? Knowing Liam, he would probably never tell her unless it was something he wanted her to know!

God, she wished he would come to some sort of decision concerning the business. The waiting was killing her! All she had wanted from him was a

133

straightforward yes or no, but she knew that he wouldn't be rushed, and that his decision, when it came, would be made on a practical business level, would have nothing to do with love or loyalty towards his father. Basically because he didn't feel either of those things towards his family.

And he wasn't about to come to any decision when he wasn't even here!

John came into her office later in the morning, and Juliet could see that he wanted an explanation of what was actually going on, which wasn't surprising considering Liam had walked in and more or less taken over William's office—at the least!

There wasn't a lot she could really tell John; she had no idea herself what was happening. It could take Liam weeks to decide whether or not to keep the company going—which wasn't a lot of help to John, she accepted, but it was all she could offer him at the moment.

'Will Mr Liam be in for dinner tonight?' Janet asked her when she arrived home later that evening.

She had no idea what Liam's plans were for this evening; given that she hadn't seen him all day, how could she possibly know? He hadn't been into the office at all today, not even to speak to Diana. Not that the other woman had seemed concerned by his absence; she was probably used to it. Diana certainly seemed to accept working alone.

There had been no time for the two women even to take a hurried lunch together today; Juliet was back in the midst of her own work now, Diana still poring over accounts in William's office. Besides, Juliet felt a little uneasy in the other woman's company now as she was no longer so sure of Diana's relationship with Liam; he had certainly seemed defensive enough over the other woman when he'd come home last night!

'I have no idea,' Juliet replied dismissively. 'Liam doesn't keep me informed of his movements.'

'He never did.' Janet shook her head affectionately. 'He always was the more independent of the two boys.'

Boys? Juliet again found it difficult to imagine Liam as a boy.

Janet laughed at her expression. 'I can never think of him as anything else!' she smiled. 'He was a mischievous little devil.' Her face clouded slightly. 'Until Simon was born, that is.'

Juliet stiffened slightly at the mention of her dead fiancé; she had never discussed Simon with Janet. In fact, she hadn't really spoken of him since his death. Whether that was a good or bad thing she wasn't sure; she just knew that she found it too painful to talk about him.

But she was interested in this conversation in spite of herself. 'What effect did that have on Liam?' She frowned. As she did not have any siblings of her own, or any other family either, it was unknown territory for her.

Janet shrugged. 'Well, his mother died, for one thing, so that didn't help the situation. And Mr William doted on the baby, which didn't help either, so——'

'Liam and Simon didn't get on,' Juliet guessed.

'I wouldn't say that as children they didn't get on,' Janet said slowly. 'After all, Liam was five when Simon was born—already at school, with his own group of friends. It was only as they grew up that the resentment became more obvious.' She shook her head sadly. 'By the time they were both teenagers it was like open warfare!'

So Liam has been resentful of his younger brother. She had guessed from his attitude towards Simon that there had been no love lost between the two brothers, and Janet had just confirmed it.

'It was very difficult for Mr William.' Janet gave a heavy sigh. 'He loved both his sons——'

'That's debatable, Janet!' cut in a harshly angry voice, and both women turned to find that Liam had entered the house without either of them being aware of it.

Janet immediately looked flustered at being caught discussing him in that way, and Juliet had to admit that she wasn't too happy about it herself. She was sure that Liam's remarks last night about not discussing him, or his private affairs, with Diana also applied to Janet!

He strode forcefully into the entrance hall, closing the door behind him with firm finality. 'We'll have coffee in my father's study, Janet,' he told the housekeeper icily, his eyes glittering like twin blue lakes—fathomless lakes with a threat in their depths! 'The study, Juliet,' he told her coldly as he marched past, not even pausing to see if she intended following him.

He just knew that she would! Not that she wanted to, but she accepted that she probably did owe him an apology for being caught out talking about him with Janet. But it hadn't been intentional; it had just been a natural progression in the conversation.

Janet made a pained expression. 'Oh, dear,' she sighed, looking guiltily after Liam.

'Don't worry about it,' Juliet said softly, squeezing her arm reassuringly. 'We weren't doing anything wrong.' Although she doubted whether Liam saw it that way!

Janet shook her head regretfully. 'I know that look,' she said, grimacing. 'His father had one just——' She broke off awkwardly. 'Liam always was as stubborn as a mule,' she sighed. 'And he isn't going to like it that we were talking about him.'

'It will be fine,' Juliet assured her with more confidence than she actually felt; Liam was furious, and her delay in joining him wouldn't be improving his mood. 'You go and get the coffee and I'll speak to him.' She gave the older woman a comforting smile.

Janet didn't look any more convinced about Liam's mood than Juliet felt, but she went off to get the requested coffee anyway.

Juliet took a deep breath and followed Liam to the study. She almost faltered as she entered the room, finding him sitting behind the desk in William's chair, his face set in a cold, angry mask; obviously this was not going to be a pleasant conversation. Not that she had particularly expected it to be, but facing Liam across the desk like this she felt like a naughty schoolgirl who had been called in by the headmaster to be chastised for some misdemeanour!

He sat forward to rest his elbows on the desktop, lacing the fingers of each hand together in front of his face, his eyes icily assessing as he looked at her. And looked at her. And looked at her.

The silence stretched on and on, until Juliet felt as if her nerve might snap. 'For goodness' sake, Liam,' she finally bit out tautly, that feeling of being a naughty little girl still with her. 'Janet was just——'

'I'm not interested in what Janet was doing,' he cut in harshly. 'I believe I made my feelings plain to you yesterday evening!'

She swallowed hard. 'Janet just wondered if you were going to be in for dinner,' she continued determinedly. 'And one thing led to another.' She shrugged dismissively.

His mouth twisted. 'I'm sure it did. Well, in future——' his face hardened '—I would prefer it if one thing didn't lead to another!'

'Fine,' she snapped, tired of these mood swings. 'I'll endeavour not to let your name pass my lips again!'

He sat back, looking at her through narrowed eyes. 'Really?' he drawled.

Juliet suddenly didn't like the way he was looking at her; she felt uncomfortable under that appraising gaze. 'Really!' she returned—somewhat defensively, she felt.

Liam stood up slowly, moving stealthily around the desk and standing dangerously close to her. 'Never?' he challenged softly.

There was heated colour in her cheeks now, and she wanted to move. Instead, she stood her ground with great effort. Inwardly she just wanted to get away from him! What was it about this man that had this effect on her?

She met his gaze unflinchingly. 'Look, Li—Liam,' she completed firmly. 'It would obviously be better if you and I stayed away from each other as much as possible——'

'Why?' he cut in softly. 'Some of the times we've been ... close I've enjoyed very much.' His gaze moved appraisingly across her face and body.

Her cheeks were burning now, and she had to force herself not to move away. 'You know very well what I'm talking about, Liam,' she rapped out. 'You're here on business; there's no need for us to put up a pretence of getting on!'

He shrugged unconcernedly. 'But on one level we do "get on", Juliet,' he drawled huskily. 'In fact, I'm amazed at just how well...'

She knew to which 'level' he referred; it would be impossible not to know! And she wasn't amazed by it at all—stunned would be a better way of putting it!

She might not have moved away, but there was definitely a barrier going up around her! 'You won't be here for much longer, Liam, so——'

'Are you telling me or asking me?' His voice was dangerously soft now.

Her eyes flashed her irritation with this verbal game he was playing. 'Carlyle Properties is a very small fish in your large pond, Liam,' she snapped impatiently. 'Once you've seen what you need to you'll be going off to deal with your other businesses. Until that time, as I've already said, perhaps it would be better if we avoided each other as much as possible.'

'Is that what you did with your last business partner?' he taunted challengingly. 'Strange; I thought you had rather a different arrangement with my father.'

She drew in a sharp breath at his deliberately insulting tone. 'I wasn't your father's business partner,' she reminded him tautly.

'Oh, no, of course you weren't.' He nodded agreement. 'Assistant, wasn't it? Well, I suppose at his age he needed all the assistance he could—I wouldn't, if I were you,' he advised in a menacingly soft voice as her hand arched up instinctively.

Her hand was arrested in mid-action, her breathing ragged in her agitation. 'You are the most insulting man I have ever met in my life,' she finally managed to say. 'That happens to be your father you're talking about!' She glared at him for the slur he was making on a man she had cared about very much. And who had cared about her in return.

'He was a man, wasn't he?' Liam dismissed harshly.

'He was my friend,' Juliet defended. 'My very good friend.' She could have kicked herself for allowing that emotional catch in her voice; Liam wouldn't understand things like platonic love between two people who weren't actually related to each other. And now wasn't the time to enlighten him, either, as she could hear Janet approaching the study with the coffee-tray.

'Could I have a dinner-tray in my room?' she requested stiltedly of the other woman as she entered after knocking briefly on the door. She studiously avoided looking at Liam; she was so angry and upset that she might say something completely unforgivable if she looked at him again.

'I have something I wish to discuss with you, Juliet,' Liam told her coldly before Janet could answer.

She still couldn't bring herself to look at him; she needed some time and space away from him. 'Can't it wait until morning?' she said abruptly.

'No. It can't,' he answered uncompromisingly. 'It's business,' he added curtly as she still looked mutinous.

Juliet drew in a ragged breath. Liam had the upper hand in this situation, and he knew it. When it came to the future of Carlyle Properties—something William had entrusted to her—then she had no choice...!

She nodded. 'I'll join you for coffee after dinner,' she conceded, at last looking up at him—and then wishing she hadn't! Liam had a way of looking at her that made her feel so—so... It was very uncomfortable, feeling that someone disliked you as much as Liam seemed to dislike her!

Although dislike possibly wasn't the right word. As he had admitted, on one level they did get on, and Liam obviously resented that fact. He couldn't dislike her because he wouldn't really allow himself to get to know her, but he did resent the effect they had on each other. As she did.

'Very well,' he accepted icily, obviously not too happy with the compromise, but willing to let it go by because of Janet's presence. 'Ten o'clock, in the study,' he added hardly.

'Very well,' she acknowledged distantly.

'And make sure she does have a tray in her room, Janet.' He turned to the housekeeper. 'Juliet has a habit of forgetting that her body needs food!' he added drily.

Juliet gave him a narrow-eyed look before turning on her heel and abruptly leaving the room.

'He had to have the last word,' she muttered to herself disgruntledly as she went up the stairs. She hoped his dinner gave him indigestion! It was the least he deserved, because she surely wasn't going to enjoy her own food, no matter what Liam might have instructed to the contrary!

Ten o'clock came around all too quickly as far as Juliet was concerned. She did eat some of the delicious dinner which Janet brought up for her, just the smell of the beef Wellington making her feel hungry—mainly, she suddenly realised, because she had forgotten to eat lunch. It certainly had nothing to do with what Liam had said to her!

Why did he bring out such childish rebellion in her? she wondered heavily. She had lived her life quite sedately for the last seven years, and in a few short days Liam had reduced her to an emotional see-saw, one minute so angry with him, the next unable to resist being in his arms. She would be glad when he had gone out of her life again!

But would she . . . ?

Yes, Liam evoked emotions she hadn't felt for some time, emotions she wasn't altogether comfortable with, but at least she had been alive, totally alive, since first meeting him.

She couldn't be falling in love with him . . . ? Not with Liam of all people!

She felt angry in his presence, irritated, apprehensive occasionally, but those other emotions—of anticipation of seeing him again, the pleasure she had known in his arms, the fact that she felt so alive in his company—what did they mean? They

couldn't mean she was falling in love with him—
was already in love with him...

God, it was gone ten o'clock now; if she didn't
go downstairs soon he would——

'A question of the mountain coming to
Mohammed?' Liam drawled as he entered her
bedroom unannounced.

After the recent thoughts she had been having
about him, being alone with him in her bedroom
was the last thing Juliet wanted!

She stood up abruptly from where she had been
seated at the table in front of her bedroom window.
'I was just about to come downstairs and join you,'
she told him stiltedly as she crossed the room to
stand pointedly beside the open doorway.

Liam shrugged, making no effort to move. 'I'm
here now,' he dismissed easily. 'We may as well stay
here.'

No, definitely not! 'Business is better discussed
in the right surroundings,' she insisted determinedly.

His mouth twisted mockingly. 'So I seem to remember you telling me once before,' he said, reminding her of the evening at the hotel in Majorca.
'I rarely deal in offices, Juliet,' he continued drily.
'More business is settled over a good meal, or in a
bedroom,' he added pointedly, 'than has ever been
achieved in a boardroom!'

His meaning, concerning the bedroom, wasn't
lost on Juliet, and she didn't like the implied insult
one little bit! 'I would prefer to go down to the
study,' she told him distantly, grey eyes unblinking
as she met the challenge in his gaze.

'Whatever,' he finally shrugged. 'It's really totally
irrelevant to me.'

She would imagine most things were that he didn't think directly affected him. And, as she knew from experience, Liam would say what he had to say no matter what the surroundings.

'The study it is, then,' she said determinedly, unconcerned with what he might think of her stubbornness.

'After you.' He stepped back in an exaggerated movement to allow her to pass him.

Juliet kept her head held high as she went to walk past, and looked up in startled surprise as he stepped in front of her, her eyes widening in trepidation as she saw the look on his face.

'What is it about you?' he muttered, almost to himself. 'I have every reason to dislike you, and yet . . .' He shook his head in self-disgust. 'What do you use, Juliet? Spells and magic potions?' he added harshly.

She swallowed hard, unable to move, held captive by the intensity of those dark blue eyes. 'I don't know what you mean.' She gave an involuntary quiver of awareness.

Liam saw her reaction to their closeness. 'Oh, I think you do.' He nodded, one hand slowly moving up to caress the length of her hair. 'I want to make love to you, Juliet!' The words were said harshly, as if the need was completely against his will.

As Juliet had no doubt it was! She felt the same attraction herself. But the difference was that she knew it just couldn't happen. Wouldn't happen!

'Liam——'

'Don't start reasoning, Juliet,' he bit out hardly, his arms moving possessively about her waist. 'I've done enough of that myself, and at the end of the day the whole damn lot goes out of the window the moment I'm alone with you!' he ground out disgustedly, the warmth of his breath stirring the hair at her temples.

There was no way she could escape from the steel band of his arms without seriously bruising herself, but she held herself as far away from him as she could, pushing against his arms. 'This is ridiculous, Liam.'

'I know that, damn you!' he muttered viciously. 'But maybe the only way to kill this thing is to make love to you!'

'You——' she got no further in her protest as his mouth came down almost savagely on to hers, demanding a response from her.

There was no gentleness in him, no caring for the bruises he was inflicting upon the softness of her skin, only forceful demand as he plundered her mouth and body with an anger that bordered on savagery.

Juliet whimpered low in her throat, her head flooded with deep, dark memories—memories that made her fight against him with every ounce of her strength.

And it was a battle she was destined to lose.

Liam was so much stronger than she, ruled by a passion he didn't even try to check as he swung her up in his arms, kicking the door shut with his foot before carrying her across the room to the bed, giving her no chance to escape as his weight came down on hers and his mouth claimed hers once again, his hands restlessly caressing the length of her body.

There was no respite to the demanding kisses. Liam seemed unaware of the low sobs in her throat, the convulsions of her trapped hands against his chest. Juliet could feel herself drowning, drowning in a sea of blackness that had no end.

'Liam, no!' she cried as she hung on to the last remnants of consciousness. 'Please, no!' This last was a begging plea, a need to be heard. 'Don't do this to me! Please . . . don't do this to me!' She was sobbing in earnest now—uncontrollable sobs that racked the whole length of her body.

He raised his head to look down at her with glazed eyes, staring uncomprehendingly at the river of tears running down her cheeks.

'Liam, please!' She looked up at him with pain-filled eyes, her face completely white, her hands clasped into defensive fists in front of her breasts, shock starting to set in too now as her body began to shake. 'P-please . . . !' she sobbed brokenly.

He frowned deeply, shaking his head as if to clear it from a fog and drawing in deep breaths of air to his seemingly starved lungs. 'Oh, God!' he finally groaned, throwing himself back on the bed beside her, his arm flung up over his eyes, as if he too wanted to shut out the memory of what had just almost happened.

Shock was setting in properly in Juliet now, and she lay rigid on the bed, unable to move, shaking too badly even to attempt to stand up, even though at this moment she wanted to put as much distance between herself and Liam as she possibly could.

'Hell!' He shot up off the bed, striding over to the window to stare down sightlessly at the driveway. 'Hell!' he muttered again, running an agitated hand through the dark blond thickness of his hair.

That was exactly where Juliet felt that he had taken her! Her numbed senses were starting to thaw, and so the pain began to feel more intense. Liam had been intent upon making love to her, with or without her co-operation. No doubt he would have preferred it with, but——

'Take that look of horror off your face!' he instructed harshly, looking at her from across the room now, very pale, a nerve pulsing in his cheek. 'I'll admit I was beyond reason for a few minutes, but I would never have actually made love to you without your consent!' He shook his head in denial of just how beyond reason he had been.

'Which I would never have given,' she returned huskily, surprised that she could articulate at all; she did feel horrified by what had almost happened.

Liam drew in a ragged breath. 'Possibly not,' he conceded icily. 'We'll never know. But what I do know,' he added quickly as Juliet was about to assure him that she certainly did know, 'is that it isn't a good idea for me to continue staying in this house.' He looked about him scathingly. 'Just a house.' He shook his head. 'And yet it's always held bad memories for me!'

And now it held even more! Juliet didn't believe that she would ever be able to enter this bedroom again without remembering what had happened here with Liam.

She sat up slowly, feeling the bruises he had inflicted on her body. 'I'll be the one to move out,' she said softly, not even looking at him, knowing she couldn't stay here any longer. It had been bad enough before, but now...!

'My father left this house to you,' Liam reminded her harshly.

She shook her head, moving like an automaton as she slipped on a pair of shoes. 'I never wanted it. I know you don't believe me, but I never wanted any of what he left me. But William felt responsible——' She broke off abruptly, turning sharply to look at Liam with stricken eyes. She had said too much; she knew she had by the narrow questioning of his eyes.

'Responsible for what?' Liam predictably prompted.

God, this had disturbed her! She would never have——

'Juliet!' he ground out forcefully.

She moistened suddenly dry lips. 'Nothing,' she denied hurriedly. 'It was nothing.'

He didn't look convinced—and Juliet had secretly known he wouldn't be. He was far too astute; he missed very little of what was going on around him. And he thought he knew her very well. He didn't, but he believed he did.

He gave her a considering look as he slowly crossed the room to stand in front of her. 'I had a question to ask you tonight, Juliet, and I believe you've just answered it for me!' he said coldly.

She looked up at him frowningly, not liking that look of disgust on his face one little bit. Why should he be the one who was disgusted? She was the one who had almost been... almost been...

Liam's mouth twisted scathingly. 'It was a cover-up, wasn't it, Juliet?' he accused, revolted. 'A

damned cover-up that cost a life——' He broke off
as Juliet rose abruptly to her feet.

If she had looked at him with horror before, it
was as nothing to the terrified despair she felt now.
How could he know so quickly? How could he
possibly have guessed the secret which she and
William had kept for so many years?

CHAPTER NINE

LIAM turned sharply away from her, thrusting his hands deep into his trouser pockets as he moved over to the window once again, as far away from Juliet as he could possibly be in this room. 'How well did you know my little brother, Juliet?' he finally rasped, his back still towards her—a back rigid with suppressed anger.

She swallowed hard. 'I told you——'

'How well, Juliet?' His tone brooked no prevarication.

She chewed on her bottom lip, looking down at her clenched hands. 'I was engaged to marry him,' she said quietly.

She sensed rather than saw Liam turn sharply to face her, and felt unable to raise her head and return the probe of his gaze. If she looked at him now, just once, he would see it all in her face. And she had kept it to herself for so long... Although it seemed that Liam now knew the truth. She still didn't understand how he could possibly know...

'You said you weren't around ten years ago, so I knew it had to be something like that,' he said disparagingly. 'You have consistently denied being intimately involved with my father, so that only left Simon. You had to have been close—very close— to at least one member of this family to have been privileged with such information. My father was an expert at burying family skeletons,' he added disgustedly.

Juliet was still caught up on the 'ten years ago'; she didn't understand what Liam meant by that. It wasn't ten years ago, it was only... Was there some mistake? Could Liam possibly be talking about something else completely? The Walters account? Was that it? Liam had said that the account was ten years old. If it was that account, what cover-up was he talking about?

She drew in a deep breath. 'It was so long ago, Liam——'

'A man died!' he bit out harshly, his eyes blazing across the width of the room. 'The compensation my father paid the family can never change the fact that Simon was completely responsible for his death. Through greed and incompetence—but mainly greed!' he concluded contemptuously.

Juliet was very pale, staring across the room at him, not having taken in any more of his words after his statement 'Simon was completely responsible for his death'. Simon had killed someone? How? Why?

'No amount of money can make up for that,' Liam added disgustedly. 'Simon should have paid, and paid dearly, for what he did. But my father wouldn't accept that,' he said bitterly. 'Simon could do no wrong in his eyes.'

Juliet felt sick, could hardly breathe. Simon had *killed* someone? And William had known about it, had covered it up, had continued to hide that knowledge, had taken it to his deathbed? God, no wonder...

'You were going to marry a man who as good as committed murder,' Liam continued remorselessly. 'Oh, my father doctored the file; Simon's signature doesn't appear on a single one of the documents. But we both knew, once the whole damned building had collapsed and crushed that poor devil beneath it, that Simon had used inferior materials while falsifying the invoices to look otherwise; that he had pocketed the money he saved.

'But, even though I told my father that, he refused to accept it as the truth, accused me of being bitter towards the blue-eyed boy he considered my brother to be.' Liam's face was full of disgust. 'That's when I walked out,' he ground out harshly. 'I didn't want any more to do with this family, wanted no part of them!'

So now she knew the secret of Liam's alienation from his family. God, it was so much worse than she could ever have imagined. Simon ... Oh, God, how could he have done that? And how could William have——?

'But my father knew it was the truth,' he bit out coldly. 'Otherwise, why did he change all the documents in that file and put his own signature on them? Still protecting Simon! And you've carried on doing the same thing!' He shook his head in revulsion.

Juliet looked up at him with stricken eyes. 'I didn't know anything about that,' she choked. 'I didn't know!' she repeated desperately when she could see the cold scepticism in Liam's eyes.

'How can you say that?' he said, scornfully disbelieving. 'My father obviously felt some sort of responsibility towards you—you've already ad-

mitted as much!—and that responsibility can only
have been because you knew you were marrying a
man capable of allowing another human being to
die because of his own greed. It's commonly known
as blackmail, Juliet,' he added contemptuously.

Juliet was still too shocked even to attempt to
defend herself on that last accusation. What had
Simon *done*? How could William have protected
him in that way? God, no wonder William had
seemed so pleased when Simon seemed to be settling down and getting married! But later—William
had to have known later.

Liam was right; William had felt a responsibility
towards her, but that was because of his own guilt
at protecting Simon for all those years, not because
of anything she had said or done. But the coldly
contemptuous look on Liam's face told her that he
wasn't about to believe any explanation she gave
him. And the truth was still too painful for her to
talk about.

'I'm moving out of this house, Juliet,' Liam told
her harshly. 'As of now! I should never have come
back here in the first place.' He shook his head self-
disgustedly as he looked around him. 'It's a house
full of lies and destruction. And the sooner I'm
away from it again, the better I'll feel!' He strode
purposefully over to the door.

Juliet just looked at him, still too stunned by
everything he had said to try to defend herself. But
he was right about this house; it was full of lies and
destruction, and she no longer wanted to be here
either!

'Liam——'

'Not now, Juliet,' he snapped coldly, swinging the door open. 'I need to get away from here—from you!—so that I can start to think straight once again!' He slammed the door forcefully behind him, the room reverberating with the sound.

Juliet was too shocked to move, too numb to cry. Oh, William, what did you do? she silently cried inside herself.

She was very pale when she entered her office the next morning. She hadn't spent the night sleeping; she had been thinking about what she intended doing with the rest of her life. Because she didn't intend staying on at Carlyle House, or Carlyle Properties. She had loved William as a father, had felt grateful to him for what he had done for her, had felt a responsibility towards the company because of the care he had shown towards her. But all that had changed last night with Liam's revelations.

William had known exactly what Simon was capable of and had chosen to protect him. And in the end they had both paid a price for that protection.

She owed William nothing. In her, she had decided during the dark hours of the night, William had seen a way for his son to settle down to respectability, hoping, she was sure, that marriage would calm and tame his son in a way he had never been able to do. But, even at the end, Simon had proved that had not happened; his death had been as violent as it had been unnecessary.

Her love for Liam, she had also decided, was futile, absolutely futile, and perhaps it was the price she would have to pay for her own silence where Simon was concerned.

And so now, with her last ties with the Carlyle family broken, was the time for her to leave. Oh, she didn't intend just disappearing; she had legalities to sort out before she left, concerning both the house and the business. But once she had dealt with those...

Where she would go she had no idea. Just as far away from here—and Liam!—as she could possibly be!

God, no wonder Liam was so contemptuous of both his father and Simon. And her...

It was that contempt from Liam which she couldn't cope with. There had been so much pain, but his contempt towards her was unbearable.

'So nice of you to turn up!'

Juliet turned guiltily at the harsh sound of his voice. She had just been about to enter her office when the door opposite hers had opened. Just her luck that it was Liam.

She knew she was late, by almost an hour, but she just hadn't felt motivated to arrive here at all this morning. The business she had been trying so hard to save had been built on lies. On a man's death. She could guess, from Liam's accusations last night, exactly what had happened ten years ago; Simon had been in charge of the Walters project, had cut corners, and used inferior materials so that the remainder of the budget might go into his own pocket. And a man had died because of it.

Simon had had no need to do anything so potentially dangerous, because William had always given him everything he had ever asked for, which made his crime doubly horrifying. No wonder Liam had found it impossible to stay, either with his family or the company.

As she did now.

'A late night doesn't entitle you to work part time,' he derided harshly, looking down his arrogant nose at her. 'Neither does being a half-owner,' he added insultingly.

'I——'

'Although from the look of you perhaps you shouldn't be here at all!' He looked her up and down scathingly, his contemptuous gaze finally resting on the paleness of her face. 'What's the matter, Juliet?' he taunted hardly. 'Did the truth hurt?'

Her eyes filled with tears. What Liam had told her last night hadn't just hurt her, it had deeply shocked and disgusted her, and had seriously altered how she felt towards William. And as for Simon...

'Oh, for God's sake!' he rasped impatiently at the sight of those unshed tears. 'Why do you always make me feel like a heel?' he said disgustedly. 'I got out of this family once, Juliet; you were the one to bring me back! How did you expect me to feel towards William and Simon?' he added exasperatedly. 'Just because they're both dead, they aren't suddenly going to become nice people in my eyes; I knew them for what they were, and I wanted no part of them!'

Neither did she, now that she knew what William had done. It had been his own guilty conscience that had made him be so nice to her; he had known all the time exactly what sort of person Simon was.

'We need to talk, Liam.' Her voice was husky from the tears she had cried long into the night. 'But now isn't the time to do it.' She looked around them pointedly; the corridor was far from private, although she acknowledged that so far they hadn't been interrupted; probably Liam's raised voice had been heard by any employees who might have wanted to come down the corridor, and they had considered it the wrong time to do so! 'Could I talk to you later this evening?' There was none of her past anger and resentment towards this man in her voice; all the fight had gone out of her.

'At the house?' His voice was sharp, his eyes narrowed.

'No!' She held back a shudder with effort.

She had already packed her things—that was another reason why she had been late this morning—and she intended to return to Carlyle House only once more herself, in order to pick up her suitcases.

She drew in a deep, controlling breath. 'Perhaps we could have dinner?' she suggested more calmly.

'A dinner at which I would have to sit and watch you not eat!' He dismissed her words scathingly with a negative shake of his head.

'A drink, then,' she conceded agitatedly, knowing that he was right about the dinner; she didn't think that she would be able to swallow any food even if she tried to. 'Just somewhere where we can talk privately.' She looked up at him pleadingly.

His expression remained hard. 'What's so private that we can't talk about it here, Juliet?'

'I——' She broke off abruptly as John Morgan walked down the corridor towards them.

'OK, point taken,' Liam muttered as he too saw the other man's approach. 'But this had better be good, Juliet,' he added impatiently. 'I have a damn sight more on my mind at the moment than Carlyle Properties!'

She didn't know whether he would consider it good at all; she intended telling him that she wanted no further part of the business or Carlyle House; that they were both his. And as he didn't seem to want them either . . .

'John,' he greeted the other man abruptly. 'Is it me or Juliet you want? Or is that a stupid question?' He looked at the two of them speculatively.

The implied insult went over John's head as he gave Liam a puzzled look, and as the younger man was due to marry his long-standing girlfriend the next month that wasn't so surprising. 'Juliet, actually,' he replied.

'Naturally,' Liam drawled. 'I'll leave the two of you to it, then. We'll leave together at five-thirty, Juliet; will that do? We can sort out where we're going then,' he added challengingly.

It was far from ideal, because it meant that she would have to go back to the house to pick up her things after she had spoken to him, but in the circumstances . . . 'That's fine,' she agreed softly.

'Good.' He somehow managed to convey the point that he really didn't care whether it was fine with her or not; if she wanted to talk to him privately, that was when they would do it, at his convenience, not hers.

'Five-thirty, then,' she confirmed abruptly, very aware of John's presence.

'Yes.' Liam turned and re-entered his office.

John gazed after him frowningly. 'I can't quite work him out,' he finally said slowly. 'He's been prowling up and down this corridor for the last hour, I'm sure waiting for you to arrive, and now that you have his mood doesn't seem to have improved!'

Liam might have been waiting for her to arrive, but only so that he could snap her head off for being late once she got here! It didn't actually take a lot to work Liam out; he hadn't wanted to be here at Carlyle Properties, didn't want to be here, and resented being so. She didn't doubt that it was only his curiosity that had got him to come back here at all—a curiosity that must have been more than satisfied by now! And Juliet didn't doubt that now that it had been he would very shortly be leaving. Except that she was leaving first, so he might find it a little difficult to do that.

But she wouldn't go before telling him what she was doing, even if she couldn't tell him all the reasons why.

The minutes and hours of the morning dragged by, possibly because it was her last day at Carlyle Properties and, like Liam, she didn't want to be here either. Despite what she might have originally thought, perhaps it would be best if Liam let the company fold; after what he had told her about its past, it was probably better if it did. The company was tainted.

By one o'clock she decided that she needed a break. And she didn't care what Liam had to say about her taking an hour off for lunch. What did it matter anyway? She wouldn't be here at all tomorrow!

It was just her luck that Diana was walking down the corridor as she left her office. The other woman gave her a warm, friendly smile. 'Off for lunch?'

Lunch hadn't actually entered into her plans; just an hour out in the fresh air somewhere would be one hour less that she had to spend here. 'Yes,' she answered abruptly, not quite meeting the other woman's gaze.

Diana's face brightened. 'I'll come with you, shall I? Lunch the other day didn't really count!'

Juliet didn't want to spend an hour with this woman, trying to act sociably. She didn't want to spend an hour with anyone at the moment. 'I——'

'I'll just tell Liam we're going,' Diana said, cutting lightly across her objection. 'I'll only be a moment,' she promised before entering the office she and Liam had been sharing for the last couple of days.

Juliet could imagine that Liam was going to be absolutely *thrilled* at the idea of her taking his personal assistant away for an hour, especially as she herself had been in an hour late already this morning! It wasn't even as if she wanted the other woman to come with her...

Liam's explosion wasn't long in coming!

'What do you mean you're going to lunch with Juliet?' he snapped angrily. Diana had left the office door slightly ajar when she'd gone back into the office.

Juliet cringed at the anger in his voice, wishing she were anywhere but standing in this corridor, an unwilling listener to the exchange. She didn't hear Diana's quietly spoken reply, only Liam's response.

'How else should I feel?' he challenged harshly. 'I'm wasting precious time even looking at this damned company, when I have interests of my own that need attention. You're pregnant, and—— God, I'm sorry, Diana!' His voice had softened in his hurried apology. 'I know you feel badly enough about that already. Don't worry, we'll work something out. It isn't the end of the world. Tom will come round. He'll understand. Oh, God, Diana, don't cry; you know I don't know what to do when you cry! Diana...'

Juliet didn't stay to hear any more, but turned and walked in a daze from the building, sure that she had been forgotten by both Diana and Liam. Interests of his own that needed attention, Diana pregnant, her husband Tom would understand. It all added up to one thing: Diana was pregnant with Liam's child!

Juliet was stunned, totally shocked; she sat in her car for several minutes, unable to move.

What had she expected, hoped? That somehow during her conversation with Liam this evening she might have been able to salvage something, some sort of relationship with him?

God, she did love him. And he was having an affair with a married woman—a woman who was now expecting his child. What a mess!

How she drove back to the house she never knew afterwards; she couldn't recall the journey at all. But she knew, after the conversation she had just heard, that she couldn't return to Carlyle Properties, that she couldn't see Liam again. The only course left open to her now was to collect her things and go. She would leave a note for Liam in his father's study explaining what she was doing, and saying that he would hear from her lawyer concerning the business and house. There was no way she could actually talk to him herself now. Whatever awareness there had been between them, and no matter how she might feel about Liam, she had no part to play in his life.

As he had no part to play in hers...

A perplexed-looking Janet met her in the hallway as she entered the house. 'Miss Juliet, I've seen the suitcases in your room...' She frowned heavily. 'Are you going away on holiday?'

She was sure that the older woman must have realised that all of her things were packed in those two suitcases—everything she wanted to take with her, which was really only clothes and a few personal things. She wanted nothing that any of the Carlyle family had ever given her.

'Not a holiday, Janet,' she told the other woman gently. 'I'm leaving the house for good.'

The older woman looked stricken. 'But——'

'It's for the best, Janet.' She squeezed the other woman's arm reassuringly. 'I think we both know that I should have left seven years ago when—well, after Simon died.' She shook her head. 'I just wasn't feeling strong enough to make the break then.'

'Would you care to explain that remark?'

Both women spun round at the sound of Liam's voice. He stood in the doorway behind them, his expression grim.

Juliet just stared at him. How had he got here?
She hadn't heard the car in the driveway, but she
supposed he must have driven here. Had he known
she was here too?

'Well?' He looked at her challengingly, closing
the door firmly behind him.

She couldn't even remember what she and Janet
had been talking about when he arrived, so shocked
was she by his presence here!

'Why weren't you feeling strong enough to leave
seven years ago?' he prompted harshly, blue eyes
narrowed.

There was so much anger in this house—always
had been, Juliet realised now. 'My fiancé had just
died,' she answered quietly, not quite able to meet
the intensity of that probing gaze.

'Simon?' Liam said scornfully. 'Was he really any
loss to anyone?'

'Master Liam!' Janet gasped in a shocked voice.

He looked at her slightly regretfully. 'I'm sorry,
Janet, but you know that there was no love lost
between my brother and myself; we just didn't have
anything in common, except the same parents. If
we hadn't been related, we would have disliked each
other intensely the first time we met.' He shook his
head disgustedly. 'Simon was a spoilt child
who grew up into a spoilt, destructive man, a man
who felt—God knows why!—that the world owed
him something.'

He had so perfectly described the Simon whom
Juliet had come to know as the real Simon, not the
Simon she had imagined herself in love with. She
had thought he was wonderful, a golden-haired

Adonis, and miraculously he had seemed to find her equally attractive.

But it had all been a lie, a deception for his father's benefit; Simon hadn't really loved her at all, had just been trying to prove to his father what a steady, responsible adult he had become, so that William would retire and leave the business in Simon's complete control. She knew now, after what Liam had told her of the past, exactly why William had had reason to doubt that!

Janet shot her a concerned look. 'I don't think it helps anyone to dwell on the past, Liam,' she told him quietly.

'The past created the present,' he rasped harshly.

'The past is dead,' the housekeeper insisted firmly. 'Along with your father and Simon.'

A spasm of emotion crossed Liam's face at those words, but it was too fleeting for Juliet to be able to gauge what it was. 'But my father made sure, by leaving me half control of the company on his death, that I would have to come back here,' he bit out angrily.

Janet shook her head. 'You didn't have to come back, Liam. It would have been easy enough just to sell your shares; something inside you must have wanted to come back,' she pointed out softly.

His mouth twisted. 'My curiosity was aroused, I'll admit that,' he said grudgingly. 'Even more so once I had actually met Juliet. She wasn't quite what I had expected.'

And had expected from the information he had had on her before he had even arrived in Majorca! 'What *did* you expect, Liam?' She frowned, able to guess, from the things he had said to her since they had first met, exactly what he had thought! She had lived with his father, had been left a half-share in the company; it was obvious what he had surmised about the relationship. And he was wrong, so very wrong. As she had been too, she now knew, but for different reasons.

Liam looked at her coldly. 'Not the waif-like creature you turned out to be!' he rasped. 'I thought my father went in for more ... shapely women!' he added insultingly.

Juliet gasped, looking concernedly at Janet, sure now, even though she had never realised it while William had been alive, that the other woman had cared for him very much. And Liam was the one who had first pointed that out to her, which made his insult to her doubly hurtful.

Janet had stiffened, looking censoriously at Liam. 'That is enough, Liam,' she said steadily. 'William was a good man, and I won't stand here and listen to you insult him.'

He ran an agitated hand through the dark blond thickness of his hair. 'I know how you felt about my father, Janet.' His voice had softened. 'But it doesn't change the fact that he always protected Simon, made excuses for his behaviour, when Simon should have been made responsible for his own actions.'

'William knew that,' Janet said wearily, suddenly looking old, her shoulders stooped, her face lined with grief. 'In the end he knew that only too well, Liam.' She straightened slightly. 'And he paid a high price for loving Simon too much and turning a blind eye to his behaviour. Everyone did. Including Juliet,' she added, with a regretful look in her direction.

Juliet paled, her eyes darkly pleading as she returned the other woman's gaze.

Liam's mouth twisted. 'From what I can see Juliet was very well . . . rewarded for turning a blind eye to Simon's behaviour,' he said insultingly.

Janet shook her head. 'Liam, you don't know what you're talking about,' she said. 'And perhaps it's time you did,' she added, with another regretful look in Juliet's direction.

Juliet's eyes were huge in the paleness of her face. 'Please, Janet, don't,' she pleaded, tears welling up in her eyes.

'Juliet, I've always understood how you felt about this subject.' The other woman gently touched her arm. 'And it isn't something the two of us have ever discussed. I told William I thought you needed to talk it over with another woman rather than building it all up inside you, but he didn't seem to think you would welcome the intrusion.' Janet sighed. 'In retrospect I think he was wrong.'

'It's all in the past, Janet.' Her voice was pained.

The older woman shook her head. 'It affects the present.' She glanced across at Liam. 'And if I'm not mistaken it's causing a problem between the two of you.'

Juliet gave a slightly bitter laugh. 'There's no problem between Liam and me, Janet; we just don't like each other!' She knew that, for her own part, it was a lie, but if she salvaged nothing from this situation she at least needed her pride to be able to walk away.

'You see, Janet,' he bit out caustically, 'there's no problem; Juliet and I both know where we stand.'

'Utter nonsense,' the housekeeper dismissed impatiently. 'I've watched the two of you together; you like each other well enough—more then well enough, from the little I've seen!' she added knowingly, causing Juliet's cheeks to blush with embarrassment. 'It's time for the truth, Juliet,' she told her gently. 'Past time, I would have said,' she added firmly.

'What good will it do?' Juliet reasoned agitatedly. She didn't want Liam to know about the past! It was over, gone forever; talking about it would change nothing.

Janet shook her head. 'Perhaps none,' she conceded heavily. 'But it's time the ghosts in this house were laid to rest.'

Juliet looked at her, at the pain in Janet's face, knowing that this woman had her own share of pain from the past to cope with. Maybe it was time all the truth was told. Then they could all move on, Liam back to his own world, Juliet in search of hers. Because the truth would push her and Liam even further apart...

'If we're going to have this talk I suggest we all go into the sitting-room,' Liam said briskly. 'We may as well at least be comfortable.'

Juliet didn't think being comfortable was going to make the next few minutes any easier. Quite frankly, she would rather not have this conversation at all!

'So,' Liam prompted when they were all seated. 'What is this momentous revelation you want to make concerning my brother, Janet?' he said mockingly. 'Believe me, nothing you could tell me about him would surprise me!'

The housekeeper frowned. 'Probably not,' she agreed. 'But before I talk about Simon I want to dispel one other myth you seem to have made up in your mind. Juliet and your father were never anything more than friends. I know that,' she added firmly as Liam would have made some scathing comment, 'because your father shared my bed every night for the last twenty years of his life. Yes, Liam.' She gave him a rueful smile. 'I know you always suspected. Well, now I'm telling you that your suspicion was correct. I loved William. And he loved me.'

Liam frowned. 'Then why...?'

'Didn't we marry?' Janet finished knowingly. 'Because I wouldn't marry him. Oh, not because I didn't love him enough. Never that,' she added emotionally. 'But I was the housekeeper here, not the mistress.'

Liam stood up forcefully. 'From the sound of it you were mistress in everything but name! My father should have——'

'Your father respected my decision, Liam. He never understood it, but he respected it,' Janet said quietly. 'I was happy with the way things were; to have changed them would have put added pressures on us—pressures I felt were unnecessary. So you see, Liam, I do know what I'm talking about when I say William was only ever like a father to Juliet.' She smiled ruefully at him again.

Juliet could see that Liam found the relationship between his father and Janet difficult to understand, and she had to admit that it wasn't something she could have accepted in a relationship herself. But, as Janet had rightly made clear, it had been *their* relationship, and they had obviously both been happy with it.

Liam frowned across the room at the housekeeper. 'But when he died you were left with nothing,' he pointed out impatiently. 'A wife in everything but name!' He shook his head disgustedly. 'It may have been your decision, Janet, but the outcome is totally unacceptable. To me, at least.' He looked frowningly at Juliet.

She swallowed hard. 'I——'

'Now don't either of you feel concerned about the way William's will was worded,' Janet interrupted dismissively. 'I knew about it, we talked about it; he wanted you both to have what was left to you. And William provided for me a long time ago,' she explained softly. 'I'm well taken care of, believe me,' she added as Juliet still looked concerned and Liam frowned darkly.

'But——'

'This isn't what's important, Liam,' Janet said firmly, cutting into his protest. 'That situation was dealt with long ago, to the satisfaction of everyone involved. I only mentioned it because it's relevant to Simon. And the night he died,' she added quietly, giving Juliet a concerned look.

Juliet stiffened as Simon was brought back into the conversation. She didn't want to talk about him now—wasn't ready to talk about him. Would never be ready to talk about him. Especially to Liam!

She stood up abruptly. 'Janet, I——'

'Liam has to know the truth, Juliet,' the older woman told her regretfully. 'Too much damage has been done already. Both of you have to let the past go. And the only way to do that is to talk about it.'

Juliet was having trouble breathing. To talk about the past would bring it all back, and it had taken her such a long time to control the pain that it gave her.

'William, as usual, was with me the night Simon died,' Janet continued determinedly. 'We both heard the screams,' she added emotionally.

Liam frowned. 'What screams?'

Juliet knew what screams. She had had nightmares for months afterwards and had woken up in the night to the sound of the same screams. Her own...

'Janet, please...!' she said brokenly, her breathing ragged, tears clogging her throat.

The older woman shook her head. 'I can't remain silent any longer, Juliet. It would be wrong. Too many people have already been hurt. And now you're running away——'

'Running away?' Liam echoed sharply, looking at Juliet with narrowed eyes. 'What do you mean?' he prompted Janet.

'Juliet's suitcases are upstairs,' she explained. 'She was about to leave when you arrived home.'

Liam was still looking at Juliet. 'You were going to leave without even telling me?'

She moistened dry lips. 'I was going to tell you this evening, but——'

'But for some reason you changed your mind,' he derided harshly.

She had changed her mind because she had heard him discussing his affair with someone else! She loved this man, and leaving him was the last thing she wanted to do, but what choice did she have?

'Yes,' she acknowledged heavily. 'I changed my mind.'

His mouth tightened angrily. 'You——'

'Liam, seven years ago, on the night he died, Simon tried to rape Juliet!' Janet burst in agitatedly.

Juliet felt the colour fade from her cheeks. No one had ever... No one had ever said those words before.

Simon had tried to rape her.

CHAPTER TEN

'Now do you understand?' Janet said impatiently to Liam as she rushed to Juliet's side, helping her to sit back down in the chair.

'It's all right, Juliet,' she soothed gently, sitting on the arm of the chair to hold her in her arms. 'We should have talked so long ago.' She cradled Juliet in her arms as the tears began to flow. 'William thought it best if I left you to deal with it in your own way. But you haven't dealt with it. How could you, after what Simon did?' Her voice sharpened angrily with an anger directed towards the man who had hurt Juliet in this way.

What Janet had said had hurt her, had brought back all the memories of that awful night, but what had really hit her so hard was Liam's reaction to it. She had been looking at him when Janet had made her statement, and his initial response had been a look of total disgust! She had no idea what had followed on from that; she hadn't been able to look at him again.

What was he thinking? That she must have encouraged Simon, led him on, teased him, and then perhaps changed her mind? It hadn't been anything like that!

She sat back in the chair, closing her eyes, shutting out the other two people in the room, not wanting to look at either of them. If she didn't look at them, they couldn't see into her eyes, into her innermost soul.

It had been cold and snowy that night seven years ago. She had dined alone with William, the two of them talking about the arrangements for her Christmas wedding to Simon in four weeks' time, Simon having telephoned earlier to say that he had to go to dinner with a business acquaintance. It had never bothered Juliet when Simon called with these last-minute arrangements; she had accepted that he had a business to help run, and that very often that included being sociable with clients.

She was lying in bed reading when she heard Simon's car in the driveway, and the front door opening a couple of minutes later. She was relieved to hear him return safely, having been worried about him driving on the icy roads, and got up to put on her robe, intending to go down and have a nightcap with him before they retired for the night to their respective bedrooms.

She had only just picked up her silken robe when her bedroom door was suddenly thrown open. Turning with alarm, she relaxed slightly when she saw that it was Simon standing there, although a frown furrowed her brow when she saw how bedraggled he looked, his blond hair wind-swept, his tie pulled loosely down his chest, his shirt collar unbuttoned, and a red splash of colour down the front of his white shirt.

'You're hurt!' she said anxiously, crossing the room to his side, reaching out to touch his chest where the mark was. 'Have you been in an accident?' She panicked slightly. 'What——?' She broke off, her concern turning to puzzlement as she realised that the red mark wasn't blood, as she had initially assumed it was.

'It's lipstick,' Simon supplied tauntingly as he saw her frown.

Her hand fell away from his chest as she took a step backwards. 'Lipstick?'

'God, you're an innocent!' he said scornfully as he brushed roughly past her into the room. 'You haven't really believed that I've been to business dinners all those evenings I've been out, have you?' He looked at her pityingly.

Of course she had believed him; why shouldn't she have done?

'Poor innocent Juliet.' Simon cupped a hand round the paleness of her cheek, his fingers suddenly tightening painfully against the softness of her skin, the expression on his face suddenly savage, the fumes from the alcohol he had consumed making her feel ill. 'I may be pleasing the old man by marrying you,' he rasped sneeringly, 'but that doesn't mean I don't find the charms of other women infinitely more attractive. Unfortunately I struck out tonight, so you'll have to do!' He pulled her roughly against him, his mouth grinding down against hers.

Juliet was so stunned by what he was saying that she couldn't think straight. Simon was marrying her to please his father? Other women? God, she didn't——

'For God's sake, Juliet.' Simon raised his head slightly to scowl down at her. 'It's bad enough that I have to marry you at all; you might at least show a little response and not act like a stick of wood!'

She could taste the blood in her mouth now; his mouth had come down so savagely on hers that he had split her top lip. And she was filled with such revulsion that she wanted to be sick. She pushed against him, desperately trying to free herself, pounding her fists against his chest.

His eyes glittered with challenge as he once again looked down at her, his hands tightly gripping her wrists to stop her pummelling. 'So you want to play rough, do you?' he said triumphantly. 'That's OK with me, Juliet; I like a woman with spirit!'

Juliet glared up at him. 'I hate you!' she told him vehemently. Love had turned to hate in a matter of seconds—cruelly hurtful seconds that threatened to destroy her. She just wanted to get away—from Simon, from the pain he was inflicting.

'Hate away, Juliet,' Simon grinned. 'I'll probably enjoy it more if you do.'

What followed was a nightmare, a living nightmare. Her nightgown was ripped from her body, Simon's hands and lips everywhere. Juliet wasn't even aware of her screams until her bedroom door crashed open and a panic stricken William stood in the doorway.

He took in the scene in seconds—her fear, her dishevelled state, Simon's sneeringly defiant attitude—and he came across to drag the young man from the room, their raised voices now filling the house.

And then suddenly there was silence.

And Simon lay dead at the bottom of the stairs...

Juliet felt as if reliving those terrible moments had taken a lifetime, but in reality she knew that it had just been a rush of images, memories, and that only seconds had actually passed since she had closed her eyes, or maybe a couple of minutes at the most.

And she couldn't bear to relive those moments again. Not with Janet. And certainly not with Liam.

She stood up suddenly to rush from the room, ignoring Janet's concerned cry, Liam's shout. She just kept running, running, running.

And she had kept running—from the house, from the county, from the country.

To Majorca.

To the Carlyle hotel and leisure complex. The last place anyone would think to look for her. If anyone wanted to look for her. Which she doubted.

And for the first time in years, it seemed, she relaxed totally, the darkness of the past at last put exactly there—in the past. Somehow during the next ten days of sunshine and rest it stopped being her burden to carry any more. It was Liam's now. As was Carlyle Properties.

One thing Juliet had done since coming here was to telephone the lawyer in England and instruct him to draw up the necessary papers so that she could sign all of the company over to Liam. She had also instructed him to deed the house over to Janet's name; the other woman certainly had more right to it than she had ever had. And this way Juliet would be totally finished with the Carlyle family.

Which was the way she wanted it to be.

The way it had to be.

Her love for Liam was futile, for oh, so many reasons, but the main one had to be that he would never love her in return. But breaking free of the business, the house had somehow given her ultimate freedom in everything. There was a big world out there—a world without Liam, she accepted, but for the first time she felt an anticipation about the future. Quite what that future held for her she didn't know, but loving Liam had somehow freed her from the ties of the past.

'You're standing in the way of my view.'

Juliet froze as she stood on the sea-shore. Those words. That voice. A voice that had been arrogantly self-assured the last time it had uttered those very same words, but which was gently caressing this time.

Why was Liam here? How had he known to find her here? Only he could answer those questions, she acknowledged.

She turned slowly, her hands clenched tightly together in front of her, unsure of what she was about to see.

He stood on the sand only about ten feet away from her, dressed in denims and a blue short-sleeved shirt. But it was his face that held her mesmerised. He looked older; lines were etched beside his nose and mouth, and his expression was grim. And he had lost weight; it showed in those lines on his face, the loose fit of his denims.

'Liam, what's happened?' She frowned her concern, taking a step towards him.

'You can ask me that? Simon and my father...'

Juliet had put up a silencing hand. 'Janet has told you the truth by now, I'm sure. It's enough.'

He shook his head. 'Never enough, Juliet. What Simon tried to do——' He broke off in suppressed rage. 'My father paying the price of knowing, for the next seven years, that if the two of them hadn't fought then Simon wouldn't have fallen down the stairs! God, Juliet——'

'It's over, Liam.' She sighed. 'At long last it's over. And I think it should remain that way.' She had finally come to terms with the fact that Simon had died after his attack on her, had fallen down the stairs to his death during the fight with his father. It was a burden that William had carried to his grave. But now it was over.

For several long minutes Liam returned her gaze as intently as she was looking at him, and then he nodded acceptance of what she was saying. 'You're looking good,' he murmured huskily.

She knew that the last ten days of rest and good food had had an effect; she looked tanned and healthy in the white sundress, her hair loose about her shoulders, her eyes glowing deeply grey in her glowing face. But if she looked fit and healthy Liam looked the opposite.

'We weren't talking about me——'

'Yes, we were,' he nodded. 'The last time we spoke, that's exactly what we were doing. It took me until early yesterday evening to find out exactly where you were, when your lawyer at last relented and told me where he had received his instructions from concerning the business and the house. And even then he would only say it was Majorca,' Liam added disgustedly. 'It took me another few hours of telephoning round to realise that you had actually come here. You had to know this would be the last place I would think of looking!'

Juliet swallowed hard, her glow fading slightly at his mention of 'the last time we spoke'; that conversation had concerned Simon too, and he was at last buried in the depths of her memories.

She looked at Liam frowningly. 'Why were you looking for me at all?' She sounded puzzled. 'I thought we had said all that had to be said.'

'*I* had said what I thought needed to be said,' he acknowledged self-deprecatingly. 'God, Juliet——' He broke off abruptly after she took a step backwards as he moved forcefully towards her. 'I would never hurt you.' He sighed softly as he saw her instinctive reaction. 'You've been hurt enough already!'

She moistened her lips. 'Then why are you here?'

'Certainly not to hurt you!' he groaned. 'Don't you understand, Juliet?' He ran an agitated hand through the thickness of his hair. 'I never really wanted to hurt you. Oh, I know that I did,' he admitted heavily at her sceptical expression. 'That I was damned cruel to you at times. But I was falling in love with the very last woman on earth I thought I should ever care about!'

She swallowed hard, sure that she must have misunderstood him; Liam couldn't possibly have just said that he loved her. He couldn't have done!

He looked about them impatiently. 'Juliet, could we get off this very public beach and go somewhere where we can talk privately?' he said feelingly.

She was still reeling from what he had said a minute ago. Liam loved her?

'Juliet?' he prompted uncertainly at her lack of response.

Of course they could get off this beach; if Liam was going to tell her again that he loved her, they could go anywhere he wanted them to!

'My suite?' she suggested breathlessly, unable to take her eyes off him—possibly because some part of her was still not convinced that he was actually here, certainly not that he was telling her he loved her!

He nodded abruptly. 'I haven't had a chance to book in yet, so that will be perfect.' The two of them turned to walk side by side to the hotel a short distance away, not touching, but both very aware of the other.

Juliet had managed to book one of the ground-floor suites this time, so she was able to let them in without actually going inside the hotel itself. 'Would you like a drink?' She offered him a choice from the fridge-bar.

'Maybe in a few minutes.' His gaze remained fixed on her healthily tanned face. 'If you haven't thrown me out by then,' he added ruefully.

She frowned. 'Why would I do that?'

He drew in a ragged breath. 'I've said some pretty awful things to you——'

'With justification, I think,' Juliet interrupted firmly. 'The situation, as it stood, looked very damning. You——'

'I could have tried listening more, instead of jumping to conclusions,' he cut in with self-contempt.

'I don't think so,' she said comfortingly. 'I was engaged to your brother, lived with your father after Simon's death, inherited a house and half a business on his death; I think you may have been justified in the conclusions you came up with!' She had thought about it a lot over the last ten days; what other conclusion could Liam have come to, in the circumstances, than the one he had?

Liam grimaced. 'Don't let me off the hook too easily, Juliet,' he sighed. 'As Diana has told me, only too volubly, I deserve any verbal abuse you may want to throw at me.'

Juliet stiffened at the mention of the other woman's name; she had briefly forgotten Liam's involvement with her. What difference did it make if he loved her when he was committed to the other woman?

'How is Diana?' she asked coolly.

'Not too well.' Liam frowned. 'The doctor has ordered her to stay in bed for a couple of weeks.'

Juliet moistened dry lips. 'I see.'

'She told you about the baby?' he prompted.

'Not exactly,' Juliet answered evasively, not particularly wanting to get involved in a conversation in which she would have to admit to having inadvertently eavesdropped on something that was none of her business.

Liam shrugged. 'Tom is damned furious about the whole thing, which isn't helping the situation.' He shook his head.

Juliet stared at him incredulously. 'Doesn't he have a right to be furious?' she gasped. After all, Tom's wife was pregnant with another man's baby—this man's baby!

Liam pulled a face. 'Not particularly, no. After all, he was there too; she didn't do it all on her own.'

She frowned. Was it her, or had the conversation taken a turn she just wasn't expecting?

She shook her head. 'You've lost me somewhere, Liam.' She sat down in one of the armchairs, sure that this was going to be a long conversation, and she had no intention of standing through all of it.

Liam sat down too, across the room from her. 'Tom and Diana decided years ago that they wouldn't have children. But somehow three months ago Diana's pills let her down, and now she's pregnant after all. But if she takes it easy, looks after herself and the baby, things should go OK.

'Tom is panicking because of what happened in the past. I've tried to reassure him, but he remembers what happened to Becky only too well.' He sighed. 'There's no reason why it should happen again, but I don't suppose he can help worrying.'

No, it wasn't her; she really didn't know what this conversation was about! 'Who is Becky?' she prompted impatiently.

'Diana's sister. My wife,' he added as Juliet still looked blank. 'She died in childbirth four years ago. And the baby was stillborn.'

Juliet just stared at him. And stared at him. And stared at him. She knew he had been married—he had told her so—but she hadn't known it was to Diana's sister, or that his wife had actually died. She had a lightning replay of that conversation she had heard between Diana and Liam, and it suddenly made a different sort of sense. Liam wasn't having an affair with Diana at all, and the baby certainly wasn't his; he just happened to be a member of her family, and was concerned for her and her husband. And their unborn baby.

Which wasn't surprising when his own wife and baby had died. God, how awful for him. Her own past losses had been bad enough, but to have lost both his wife and the baby...! It must have been terrible for him. Probably still was.

'I didn't know...' Juliet said weakly.

'There's no reason why you should.' Liam shrugged, obviously still finding it a painful subject. 'It was some time ago, and isn't something I particularly want to talk about. It's just a pity that it's affecting Diana and Tom's joy over their own baby.'

'Everything will be all right, though, won't it?' Juliet said concernedly; she had come to like the other woman in the short time she had known her.

'I'm sure it will, once Tom gets over the shock.' He nodded. 'In the meantime, I'm looking for a new personal assistant,' he added slowly, uncertainly. 'And as Diana pointed out to me, during one of her less verbally condemning moments, I do know someone who is more than ably qualified.' He gave her a pointed look.

Juliet blinked, returning his gaze warily. 'Me?'

'Mmm,' he acknowledged softly. 'The benefits are that the salary is good and you would have lots of time off; I work hard, but I play hard too. But there is one major drawback,' he added heavily.

Juliet was still stunned that he was actually offering her Diana's job. How could she possibly work for him, feeling about him as she did? And, if she believed what he had said to her earlier he had feelings towards her too that wouldn't be particularly conducive to a harmonious working partnership. Unless...?

'Liam, I thought you said you believed me about my relationship with your father——'

'I do!' he assured her forcefully, crossing the room to take up a kneeling position next to her chair. 'Of course I do.' He took both her hands firmly in his. 'That wasn't the drawback I was talking about,' he said impatiently. 'Although I'm not too sure, on reflection, whether it was a particular compliment to me that you should think a relationship with me would be a drawback!' He gave a dismissive shake of his head. 'What the hell? I probably deserved that! No, the drawback is that my assistant has to be a married lady.'

Juliet frowned. 'Why?'

He shrugged. 'My wife insists on it.'

'But you've just said——'

'Well, she isn't my wife quite yet.' He grimaced self-consciously. 'But I'm hoping.' He looked up at her with dark blue eyes. 'Juliet, will you marry me?'

She stared at him once again. She didn't seem to be able to do much else at the moment!

'I love you very much,' he continued pleadingly. 'I know I haven't shown that too much, but if you'll let me I would like to spend the rest of my life making up for that. For a lot of things,' he added darkly, obviously thinking of the past. 'Juliet?' he prompted as she still remained silent. 'I just want to see you smiling and happy—see the shadows leave your eyes.'

She swallowed hard. 'You also want to fatten me up,' she said inconsequentially.

'Only a little,' he conceded. 'I just want to look after you!'

'And who will look after you?' she said huskily.

'You will. If you would like to. I mean——'

'I know what you mean, Liam,' she laughed softly, sitting forward to throw her arms about his neck. 'And I would love to look after you. And have you look after me. I love you, Liam,' she told him emphatically. 'I love you very much!'

'God, I never thought I would hear you say that!' he groaned huskily, his face buried in the thickness of her hair. 'I love you too, Juliet. And I want to spend the rest of my life with you, loving you, and having you love me.'

'Yes!' she told him ecstatically. 'Yes, yes, yes!'

'I think it's a pity that Diana and Tom chose Liam John as their baby's name,' Juliet murmured as she lay on her side in bed next to Liam, playing with the dark swirls of hair on his chest.

They had just made love, wonderful passionate love, such as they had enjoyed from the first.

Liam looked sleepily replete, his arms about her as he cradled her against him. 'I was rather pleased when they decided to name him after me.' He sounded puzzled. 'I thought you were too. You certainly spend enough time cooing over him,' he teased lightly.

Diana had given birth to a healthy son only three weeks before, to everyone's delight, and Juliet had to admit that she did spend rather a lot of time at Diana's cradling the baby.

'But what are we going to call our son when he's born?' She continued to make a pattern with the hairs on his chest.

'We have plenty of time to——' Liam broke off as she gently shook her head, looking up at him, her eyes glowing. 'We don't have plenty of time?' he said slowly.

She shrugged. 'About thirty-three weeks, by the doctor's calculations,' she told him happily.

'Juliet!' Liam shot up into a sitting position in the bed. 'You had better lie down—— Oh, you are! Oh, well, we had better——'

'Calm down, Liam,' Juliet laughed lovingly. 'I'm fit, and healthy, and very happy. And our baby is going to be the same,' she assured him firmly.

He looked down at her wonderingly. 'I didn't think it was possible, but at this moment I love you more than ever.' He gathered her up into his arms. 'I love you, Juliet Carlyle, mother of our child!'

She no longer cringed at the name Carlyle. And neither would their son. Or daughter. Or both.

'What are you thinking now?' Liam grinned down at her, a much less grim-looking Liam than he used to be, their marriage of the last six months having been an extremely happy one.

'I'm thinking,' she said slowly, her arms curving up about his neck as she pulled him down to her, 'that I would like us to make love again!'

'Any time, my darling,' he laughed huskily. 'Any time!'

BRIDE'S BAY RESORT

UNLOCK THE DOOR TO GREAT ROMANCE AT BRIDE'S BAY RESORT

Join Harlequin's new across-the-lines series, set in an exclusive hotel on an island off the coast of South Carolina.

Seven of your favorite authors will bring you exciting stories about fascinating heroes and heroines discovering love at Bride's Bay Resort.

Look for these fabulous stories coming to a store near you beginning in January 1996.

Harlequin American Romance #613 in January
Matchmaking Baby by Cathy Gillen Thacker

Harlequin Presents #1794 in February
Indiscretions by Robyn Donald

Harlequin Intrigue #362 in March
Love and Lies by Dawn Stewardson

Harlequin Romance #3404 in April
Make Believe Engagement by Day Leclaire

Harlequin Temptation #588 in May
Stranger in the Night by Roseanne Williams

Harlequin Superromance #695 in June
Married to a Stranger by Connie Bennett

Harlequin Historicals #324 in July
Dulcie's Gift by Ruth Langan

Visit Bride's Bay Resort each month wherever Harlequin books are sold.

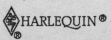

HARLEQUIN®

BBAYG

HARLEQUIN PRESENTS®

brings you

Second Honeymoon
by
Sandra Field

The second book in her great new series,
Significant Others. A series that celebrates the magical
mayhem of modern relationships and follows the loves,
lives and passionate adventures of Lucy Barnes and
her sister Marcia.

In *Beyond Reach*, Lucy was a happy bride—now she's
a runaway wife! Could her estranged husband,
Troy Donovan, be just the guy to catch her? Lucy has
turned her back on love—it hurts too much. It's hardly
an invitation for a second honeymoon, but Troy needs his
wife back or out of his system for good. He's determined
to get what he wants—even if it means seducing his
own wife....

The exciting sequel to *Beyond Reach!*

"Sandra Field pens a phenomenal love story...
 pure pleasure." —*Romantic Times*

Sandra Field's page-turning new trilogy:

*First they were strangers, then they were lovers, now
they're Significant Others!*

by Charlotte Lamb

An exciting seven-part series.

Watch for

The Sin of Envy
in

#1828 HAUNTED DREAMS

Ambrose Kerr possessed the kind of wealth and success
others could only dream about—but his happiness would
not be complete until he had Emilie!

Love can conquer the deadliest of

HARLEQUIN PRESENTS®

Available in August wherever Harlequin books are sold.

Look us up on-line at: http://www.romance.net

SINS3

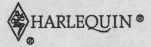

HARLEQUIN PRESENTS®

Just a taste!

Sample the exciting new story from top author
Jacqueline Baird:

#1827 *A Devious Desire*

"Wait, Alex.... Marriage is a big step—are you sure
you're ready for it? You have been a bachelor for an
awful long time."

"Marriage? Who mentioned marriage?" He let go of
her and stepped back as if he had been stung.

"I'm sorry if I misunderstood," she said softly, acting for
all she was worth. "But I'm afraid that's the only way
you'll ever get me."

Will Saffron snare Alex and get her revenge?

Available in August wherever Harlequin books are sold.

TAUTH-11